Lessons Learned

Lessons Learned

LORETTA ASATA

authorHOUSE®

AuthorHouse™
1663 Liberty Drive
Bloomington, IN 47403
www.authorhouse.com
Phone: 1-800-839-8640

This is a work of fiction. All of the characters, names, incidents, organizations, and dialogue in this novel are either the products of the author's imagination or are used fictitiously.

First published by AuthorHouse 05/27/11

ISBN: 978-1-4567-3961-4 (sc)
ISBN: 978-1-4567-3959-1 (dj)
ISBN: 978-1-4567-3958-4 (ebk)

Library of Congress Control Number: 2011901915

Printed in the United States of America

Any people depicted in stock imagery provided by Thinkstock are models, and such images are being used for illustrative purposes only.

Certain stock imagery © Thinkstock.

This book is printed on acid-free paper.

CONTENTS

Acknowledgements

First, I want to thank you Lord for blessing me with the wonderful gift of creative expression. I discovered that writing is therapeutic and it brings me great joy to be able to share my talent with others.

Secondly, for those, who had a dream but thought it worthless to pursue; just remember it was God who planted the idea in your heart to begin with. I hope this book inspires you.

Third, thank you family members and a few close friends for believing in me.

Finally, a special thanks to Helene Buckley and Orlando.

This novel has fictitious characters and has no real or current representation of actual occurrences in any shape or form. The inspiration was written from innovation and original creativity.

"To everything there is a season, a time for every purpose under heaven."

Ecclesiastes 3:1

Prologue

Spring break finally arrives at Penn State University and the 21-year-old junior decides to cut her psychology class that Thursday morning because she wanted to surprise her father, Cooper Johnson, who is the high school principal at Maple Brooke high school on his birthday. A few hours later she pulls into the parking lot of the school with a bouquet of lovely, vibrant yellow roses and a small, cuddly brown teddy bear. As she walks towards the front entrance of the school a crowd of screaming and frightened students came running towards her. She stepped aside as the panicking students rushed. Mrs. Murphy, the school secretary inadvertently bumps into her causing her to drop the teddy bear.

"I am so sorry lady." She looks up and notices the familiar face.

"What's going on, Ms. Murphy?"

"There's a student with a gun inside and your dad is inside with him. He is angry about being kicked off the football team. The police have been notified. They are on their way."

"No! Oh, My God. I've got to get inside and try to do something."

Grabbing her by the arm Ms. Murphy tries to restrain the girl from endangering herself as well as her father. However, the girl broke free and ran inside.

"Please come back." Mrs. Murphy yelled with tears coming down her cheeks; fearing the worst. Praying silently, Ms. Murphy walked to the parking lot to wait for the police and ambulance.

Meanwhile, in Cooper Johnson's office the troubled and desperate young man complains about how unfair it is to have been taken off the team in his senior year.

Overhearing all this, the girl takes off her neutral colored T-strap sandals to tip-toe to the corner near the receptionist's desk. The student remarks, "Man, you can't possibly understand what I'm going through. It's the third semester of my senior year and I got college scouts coming out to watch me play. Now by not playing, I blow any opportunity for a football scholarship."

"Jimmy, just try to calm down," replied Mr. Johnson.

"Calm down, how the heck do you expect me to do that?"

"Yes! I admit what has happened to you is unfair, but if you were doing what you were supposed to do academically, you wouldn't be in this predicament. The school's policy about maintaining a 2.0 GPA, for participating in sports, applies to every student. You aren't the exception."

"Yes, I am! You can put me back on the team, if you wanted to, but instead you'd rather not. You bastard! My life is over because of you."

"Jimmy you still have one more semester to bring up your grades. And another thing you don't want to be expelled from this ordeal or possibly sent to jail."

Just then a sound came from the front part of the office. Jimmy went to check it out and came across the girl. He violently grabbed her by her hair and shoved her into the principal's office.

"What are you doing here? We weren't expecting you until tomorrow," questioned Mr. Johnson."

"Yes, I know but dad—."

"Shut up both of you. Isn't this lovely? Father and daughter together you have the perfect family and life, but mine is all in shambles." He points the gun to Mr. Johnson and orders both of them to walk out the office.

The girl crying and terrified says, "Just let him go, please. Why are you doing this?"

"Well, answer daddy. Tell her why you won't allow me to play football with the team."

"It's a little complicated, honey."

"There isn't anything complicated about all of this you stupid old man."

"Jimmy, just let her go. You're anger is with me just deal with me only."

"Now you want to play the hero role too. You are all about yourself, aren't you?"

They walked out of the office and down the hallway. Then suddenly Jimmy demanded the girl gets on her knees and beg her father to let him back on the team.

Crying relentlessly she says, "Daddy, can you please let him back on the team?"

He hesitated to answer when suddenly Jimmy pointed the gun towards his daughter's head. Immediately Cooper's life flashed right in front of him. He couldn't bear the thought of anyone or thing harming his little girl. He went into a daze as he reminisced about the time when his little girl was only five and it was her first day at Kindergarten.

"Daddy, you don't have to stay; I'm not scared. Will you pick me up later?"

"Yes, baby I will. I love you very much and I'm here for you always."

"I love you too daddy."

He returned to the ugly reality that Jimmy still had the gun. Cooper found the strength and right moment to knock the gun out of Jimmy's hand. They started to wrestle. "Baby, get out of here!" he demanded.

"No! Daddy I won't leave you."

"Get out! NOW!"

Jimmy punched Mr. Johnson in the face. In retaliation Cooper managed to grab hold of Jimmy's neck with his hand. Meanwhile, the police had just arrived and the girl ran to the man who appeared to be in charge. Frantically she demanded he do something instantly.

"Okay, calm down," commented the police officer.

"You got to hurry before it's too late. They are in there fighting right now!"

The chief of police and a few of his officers followed her when out of nowhere a gun went off. The girl's heart rate accelerated and her breathing increased with each step leading to the main office.

She prayed to God that nobody was hurt or worse dead and perhaps miraculously that the gun shot was a misfire. When they finally reached the top of the staircase, from a distance they saw ahead a pool of blood. Heavy-heartedly, she knew that the person lying there on the floor was her father. Each step closer became painfully unbearable as she approached the scene. She knelt down beside her father's corpse and screamed out in agony and heartache. The police arrested Jimmy as he was trying to explain to them that the gun shot was an accident. The girl cried and cried like a child who had just lost its puppy. Not only did she lose her dad but a part of her as well. When the chief of police offered to take her home; she forcefully brushed him off refusing to budge. She held on tight to her father's hand and laid her head on his chest, hoping somehow that God will breathe back life into him. Looking up to the ceiling as if God himself were there she yelled, "How could you allow this to happened God? Why to my dad?"

Taking two officers to remove her from her dad's side, they put her into a police vehicle to take her home. On the ride home, she felt a deep despair in her heart; it was all because of God. She couldn't understand how a loving God could allow a good person to die so tragically. Would she ever accept the fact that her father was gone and gone forever? Today would have been her father's 50th birthday— but who knew that it will be his last.

Chapter 1

"Well done," said Melvin Rio, the VP of Marketing, as he extended his hand to congratulate his Marketing Director who did it again. That is saved one of their largest customers who have been threatening to withdraw their contract, if changes were not made to improve their ratings.

"Listen up everyone, we are closing early today and going to dinner." replied Mr. Rio.

Everyone in the office cheered and started to shut down their computers to prepare for the office dinner celebration. At the far end of the hall was the office of the Director of Marketing, Possable Johnson. She stood about 5'8"with almond shaped hazel eyes, even at age 31 she had the shape and build of a model. Her brownish rich complexion matched the color of her hair which was styled in a bun. Possable had been with KG Marketing for ten years and in her current position for three years now.

Her office was decorated with an oceanic theme sending a cool welcome to anyone who entered. She had a picture on her desk of her dog, Jordan when he was two months old. The office had a phenomenon view overlooking New York's Manhattan Bridge. Besides having a Master's degree in marketing from Penn State University, Possable worked for one of the most prestigious advertising companies in New York making well over six figures plus bonuses per year. To most, her professional life was considered exceptional and very impressive. Long hours and hard work definitely paid off. She was the center of her world and truly did not care what the other employees thought about her. She was a career-driven woman and completely happy with her life. At least she convinced herself she was. Possable was also a perfectionist who believed that all her efforts were because of her only. Her life could be perceived as absolutely perfect on the surface and there was nothing to make it go wrong.

Later that evening the staff of KG Marketing joined Mr. Rio for dinner at Tavern-on-the-Green, one of Manhattan's favorable spots to be seen and be seen. The place was packed like fans lined up to purchase Giants tickets for the Super Bowl. Thank goodness Mr. Rio's secretary made reservation for twelve. The atmosphere was loud yet inviting; medium-tone level music was playing. Servers were taking orders and rushing to tables with large trays of food. At one particularly loud table there was a group of five celebrating a friend's birthday with exchange of gifts, laughter, jokes and liquor.

Mr. Rio and his party followed the waiter to their table and were seated. After placing their orders they engaged in office conversations. The celebration was supposed to thank everyone for their hard work and dedication, but it ended up being an "all about Possable" celebration. Right in the middle of sharing her time spent at a Canadian winter carnival, she was suddenly interrupted by the ring from Mr. Rio's cell phone. He excused himself and shortly after returned with a worried expression on his face. He explained that his teenage daughter's car broke down on the Beltway and that she had no means of getting home. He wished everyone a nice long weekend, paid the bill upfront with the manager, and left. Thirty minutes later the rest of the group exchanged goodbyes and departed.

Chapter 2

Possable arrived at her 12th floor high-rise luxurious apartment in Manhattan an hour later. The weather was nasty outside, it was pouring heavily with thunder booming and lighting flashing across the sky. She switched on the light near her kaleidoscope lamp. No power. The electricity was out due to the storm. Thank God she had a candle centerpiece for her dining table, just in case of emergencies such as this. She lit the candle and dialed the number to the concierge service desk. On the second ring a friendly voice answered.

"Thank you for calling Steady Seasons" -

"Yes, hello this is Ms. Johnson at Suite 1250, I was calling to report," she interrupted herself after realizing that she was talking to an answering service, but continued with the message. "Hello, where is the concierge? Do you expect me to remain without electricity for the whole night! I am not paying $3,500 a month to sit in the dark."

She unloosed her hair from the bun and ran her hands through it, just frustrated.

A few minutes later, Jordan ran out from the bedroom ecstatic to see her. He jumped up and down, tail wagging; standing on his hind legs, looking puzzled at Possable. She patted and playfully touched him, giving him a few kisses on top of his head. While sitting on her couch she removed her shoes and relaxed. Suddenly lightning struck and Jordan barked, running to the patio window.

Instantaneously a tree tumbled down, crushing the roof of a small doughnut shop. She ran to grab her cell phone of the kitchen counter and dialed 9-1-1. She hoped not to get a recording like during an episode of one of her favorite television drama. It was when a young woman was trapped in her fourth floor apartment when a fire broke out from her downstairs neighbor's apartment.

"Hello, Hello, HELLO!" Yes, hello this is Possable Johnson speaking. I am calling to report an accident. A tree struck by lightening just fell into a little doughnut shop at 23rd and Park Place. You have got to hurry, I don't know if anyone is hurt or dead."

"Try to calm down, help is on the way," the dispatcher said right before the call disconnected.

How could Possable even consider to calm down, all kinds of thoughts were running through her mind. She kept pacing back and forward to look outside her balcony to see if the police and emergency crew arrived yet. Seven minutes later sirens from afar were growing louder and closer. She raced back to her balcony and there were four emergency ambulance vans, five police cars, and a fire truck. They all quickly responded to the scene of accident. A fire that appeared to be coming from the rear of the little doughnut shop caught the attention of one of the fire fighters. Two men raced to the rear with a water hose in hand. A few men with gas masks and body armor decided to enter from the front entrance and then *BOOM!* A huge explosion came out of nowhere. Anything and everything that was in close proximity to that explosion was dead.

Possable nearly jumped from out of her skin and opened the sliding patio glass door that lead out to her balcony. Sweat was dripping down profusely from her forehead, but the little donut shop was still standing and the once heavy, rainy weather was settling.

"It was all a dream. It was just a dream," she silently said to herself.

Suddenly the electricity came back on and the air conditioning was regenerating itself again to power on. She sat down on her red, supple leather sofa and clinched tightly onto a throw pillow relieved that it was just only a dream but at the same time lost for words to express the experience.

Chapter 3

It was 6:00 a.m. when the alarm clock in her bedroom radio sounded. She hit what she thought was the off button but ten minutes later it sounded again. She struggled to find the energy to sit up and make certain to hit the correct button this time. She could tell from the reflection of the blinds that the sun hadn't risen. She positioned herself back into bed, fluffed out her pillow, and became comfortable once more. Almost too comfortable that she quickly fell back into sleep. Not even an hour later her cell phone rang again.

"Don't people just sleep in on weekends anymore?" She answered the cell unpleasantly. "Who is this and what you want?" Jordan surprisingly jumped into her bed and startled her.

A deep voice on the other end said "It's your brother."

Her younger brother, Brandon, a middle school teacher was apparently a jokester also.

"Hey Brandon, what's going on with you?"

He chuckled as he asked sarcastically, "Are you always so pleasant in the morning?"

Possable rolled her eyes with an attitude and replied, "Why are you calling me so early in the morning anyway?" with one hand on her forehead.

"I wanted to see how you were doing. And if you're still living on top of *your* world." Possable didn't appreciate that comment. Forcefully she replied, "I am just fine. Don't be calling this early in the morning with your smart remarks. I am not in the mood. You got that?"

Brandon started to laugh hysterically. He didn't understand why she was overacting. "Alright sis, I'm sorry. Like I said before just was thinking about you and wanted to know if you were fine. I'm going to let you get back to sleep Ms. Grumpy."

Before Possable could put Brandon in his place the line went dead. "That no good, boy has a lot of growing up to do," she grunted to herself. She glanced at her clock radio it was already 9:45 a.m. The morning was getting away too quickly, she whispered to herself. Unable to return to sleep after that ridiculous conservation with her juvenile brother, she watched briefly Jordan sleeping stretched out and comfortable on her queen size bed. He looked so peaceful and absolutely adorable wrapped around like a warm blanket. She didn't want to disturb him, so she got out of bed and went to the kitchen to prepare a cup of green tea.

Later that day Possable and Jordan took a walk around the neighborhood park. Jordan was excited to see another dog and started to go crazy and whimpered. She tightens up on his leash to control and calm him down. After a few attempts, she saw that the other dog was already across the next block with its owner. She couldn't wait until Jordan grew out of his puppy stage.

The air was a bit cooler than normal that afternoon. Perhaps autumn was right around the corner. Other than leaves changing vivid colors and falling from the branches, it was also the time to decorate for the season with inviting, warm fall colors and styles in reds, oranges, purples, and shades of browns. Not to mention with the seasonal change comes Thanksgiving and Christmas. Because of the chill in the air, she hurriedly returned home with Jordan and wrapped herself in a warm cashmere sweater. She thought for a moment what on earth she was going to do for the rest of her weekend when suddenly there was a *knock, knock, knock* on the door. She peaked through her peephole and it appeared to be a pizza delivery guy.

"May I help you? Are you lost?"

"Yeah, looking for Summers residence," replied the young boy popping his gum. She definitely knew who they were because they had more drama than TNT put together.

"You want suite number 1290," suggested Possable.

The delivery boy made no attempt to say thank you and then scurried along.

The Summers on the surface appeared to be the perfect, ideal family. However, there were several incidents when Mr. and Mrs. Summers had heated arguments. The most recent was a few months ago when Mrs. Summers called the police because her drunken husband stubbornly refused to give her the keys to his spanking new, midnight blue, fully-loaded Audi convertible car.

Possable smiled and thought to herself how an intelligent, college-educated woman ended up with a loser for a husband. She checked her watched and it was quarter past five, it was time to decide what to have for dinner. A spinach chicken salad came to mind with bell peppers, tomato, red onions, shredded cheese, with a sprinkle of basil and black pepper seasoning, topped with Thousand Island dressing and croutons. She set to work in the kitchen. Preheating the oven and laid the seasoned breasts into the baking pan. From the refrigerator she got all the vegetables she envisioned for the salad and started to rinse and chop them. She poured herself a glass of white wine, placing a plate on the dining table and lit her centerpiece. She was just about to sit to enjoy her meal when she remembered Jordan needed to eat as well.

She poured out two scoops of Purina dog food into one side of his bowl inscribed with his name. The other side she filled with water. From a distance Jordan smelled the aroma. He ran into the kitchen and landed his face right into his bowl eating contently. Possable smiled, patted him on top of his head and decided to play some light music.

Standing in front of her sound system she couldn't decide if she was in the mood for Vanessa Williams or Toni Braxton. A few minutes later Toni Braxton's self-titled album won the debate. Toni was the right choice for another rainy night. She snapped her fingers into the air while softly singing and grooving in rhythm. It wasn't until the second track that she suddenly remembered she had a candle lit. Returning to her meal, an abruptly and hard loud knock startled her. The second knock was louder and harder. It was not an ordinary knock you'd expect from company visiting, but the type of knock when there's an urgent matter.

Chapter 4

Mrs. Summers stood at the door. She frantically yelled out, "Help, help me, he's going to kill me."

Possable immediately opened the door and that's when Mrs. Summers pushed her aside and then locked the door behind her.

"Mrs. Summers, I don't know what is going on, but you can't just barge in here and—." Possable noticed she was on her couch shaking and hyperventilating restlessly. Without any lights on in the apartment, other than the candle burning from the centerpiece, Possable couldn't see Mrs. Summers clearly. However, when she got closer, it was obvious her left eye was swollen. She had been beaten up pretty badly. Then all of a sudden, another bang came to the door.

"I know you're in there Rachel. Ain't nowhere for you to run."

Rachel jumped off of the sofa and moved near to the balcony. *What on earth is this woman attempting to do in my home?* Possable questioned herself.

"OPEN THIS DAMN DOOR NOW!"

Possable clumsily started to search for her cell phone in her purse to call the police. Thank God she decided to renew her contract with T-Mobile and add free weekends to the plan. She dialed 9-1-1 as she yelled to Mr. Summers, "Get the hell out of here. I'm calling the police on your trifling, sorry, wife-beating ass."

Just when the person on the other end answered, "9-1-1 please state your emergency," Rachel snatched the cell from Possable and hung up the call.

"Are you kidding me?" demanded Possable.

"No! My husband doesn't need the police on his case again. He is a respectable doctor. Besides, he is highly regarded when it comes to his dedication to his work and loyalty in the community."

"Really? I think the media will love to hear how respectful and committed a man he is beating on his wife," she said while holding up the New York Times newspaper.

Puzzled at the comment Possable asked, "Rachel, is your daughter safe? Where is she?"

"She is staying with her grandmother this weekend in Connecticut."

"Open his damn door before I kick it down. You stupid, lousy whore—you're going to be sorry!"

They both looked at each other. Possable knew calling the police was the right thing to do especially after witnessing Rachel's abused face and fear in her eyes. Rachel was too emotionally and tearful to notice when Possable grabbed the phone from the coffee table and started to re-dial 9-1-1. From the open window they heard police sirens. Evidently, someone else with good sense called the police.

Rachel got on her knees and started to pray that God will forgive her husband and not let the police arrest him for good this time.

"Freeze, put your hands where we can see them," an authoritarian voice from the hall demanded. Possable stood still to listen, relieved that the police were there.

"I'm Dr. Summers from Metropolitan Hospital. I'm here to check on one of my patients."

"Well, doc we got a report that there is a domestic dispute going on here and that you are making threats to kill your wife."

Now was the right opportunity to expose the good doctor with his lies. Possable and Rachel overheard Mr. Summers explain to the police that he was visiting a patient of his that couldn't come into the hospital because they had no reliable transportation. There was no way the police or anyone for that matter, could believe a story like that. He wasn't fooling anyone. The average New Yorker knows there are always money-hungry taxi drivers around to get you anywhere.

Rachel got up from her knees and walked toward Possable, smiled and thanked her for her help. Possable was perplexed and wondered if this woman was seriously ill or just very dense when she opened the door and told the police that Dr. Summers was her doctor. She continued her fabricated story saying she and her boyfriend just had a fight and she ran to her neighbor's house for help. That still didn't explain the threats that the anonymous caller claimed were made. Rachel added to the invention it was a heated argument that went on in the hallway. The police asked Rachel if she was alright, she didn't look so good with her swollen left eye now blackening. The rest of her face where her husband had hit her had already turned blue. Pressing charges was a good idea, but Rachel didn't want to. After Dr. Summers identified himself with his hospital ID badge all were convinced expect for Possable and one of the police officers. Possable thought to herself, *why is Rachel doing this, she is the victim here.*

Office Cruz, an NYPD veteran of several years, knew the whole situation didn't make sense. Before leaving the scene, he asked Possable for an explanation as to what really happened. Possable nervously smiled and simply said that she was glad to be home to help Rachel. Officer Cruz was quite a charmer. She always liked men in uniform, especially those in law enforcement.

He had a clean-cut haircut, nice smile, and a sexy goatee. She envisioned what life might be like to be involved with a 24/7 duty policy officer. He interrupted her thoughts when he said, "If you have any additional comments, or want to really discuss what happened here this evening give me a call."

He directed his men to head back to the station. Despite the fact that Rachel thought she convinced everyone with her sad story, he suggested once more that she should go to a hospital and get checked out. Rachel smiled and assured him she'd be just fine. He saw from the pain in her eyes that she wanted help desperately, but didn't know how. He gave Rachel his business card and told her to take care and if there was anything she ever needed to give him a call.

"Yeah, I'm sure she would do that, Mr. Office," rudely remarked Mr. Summers.

Officer Cruz gave him a mean dirty look as if to say 'you're going to regret ever saying that' then he headed toward the elevator. Silence and space stood between Possable and the Summers' for a minute then Mr. Summers kisses Rachel on the check and started to walk in the direction of their suite. Possable gave Rachel a disappointed look and asked her what she thinking when she lied to the cops.

Rachel softly responded, "Life has no guarantees and I refuse to go back to the way my life used to be before I met my husband." She then boldly walked away and opened the door to her apartment. Possable stood in the hallway bewildered by Rachel's comment and wondered what really happened here tonight. She entered her apartment, tossed her cold dinner in the garbage, blew out the candle and went to bed.

Chapter 5

2:00 a.m. Sunday morning. Possable kept tossing and turning, her mind was uneasy. She finally gave in and sat up in her bed angrily. Her whole night was restless trying to cope with the whole Rachel incident. She just didn't understand why Rachel lied for that stupid so-called noble Dr. Summers and why on earth she went back home with him. She got out of her bed, changed out of her silk red pajamas and put on a cotton terry sweat suit. Grabbing her keys and purse she locked the door to her suite and hopped into her Infiniti FX for a night cruse. Hopefully, it would help clear and ease her mind. The time on her dashboard showed 2:15 a.m. and the rain had stopped. Huge fluffy, white clouds hugged the night sky and a full moon accompanied the stars. Jazz music started to play just as soon as she started the ignition. It was just the right music to boost her low mood as she cruised down the streets of New York. People as usual were still out and about partying to their loud music playing from their cars' stereos or others were just sitting outside their homes drinking, smoking, and having good conversations.

"I love New York," she said as a smile came across her face not to mention that traffic was better around this time also. After driving a while she felt a craving for something hot to eat. That something ended up being a breakfast sandwich with hash brown and coffee. She parked and ate right there along with other drivers who had the same idea. Definitely, after that nice drive and delicious early breakfast she focused on getting back home and in bed under warm and snuggly comforter and sheets.

Chapter 6

After several rings, disturbing her sleep she finally reached her cell to put it on vibrate, but the ringing wasn't coming from her cell phone but the landline in the living room. Nonetheless, it was probably Brandon calling again to be a nuisance. Ignoring the call, she tried to get comfortable again by cuddling with her pillows. Five minutes later the freaking landline rang again, she stubbornly kicked her bed covers off, goes to the living room and snatched the phone from the base.

"Hello, what the HELL do you want Brandon?"

Silence was on the other end of the line.

"Excuse me? This is your mom, Possable. I was calling to see how you are doing."

"Oh my—mom I am so sorry. I thought you were Brandon."

"The last time I checked I had big hips and two real breasts." They both laughed in unison.

"Hey baby girl, sorry to call so early. Just was thinking about you and wanted to know when you going to come on down and see your mom."

"Mom, it's been crazy lately at work, I don't even have time for a social life anymore."

"That's not good, sweetie you need time off from being a director."

"I know mom, also the plan is to be in my own house by December."

"Now you know, I work for one of the largest real estate companies in the east and I've got connections. Let me know if you need my help."

"I'll let you know if I do and besides you have your hands full with your Eric."

"Yes! Things between us are going very well. By the way, lately Brandon has been attending church often. Plans always go well when God is in your—."

"Mom I really don't want to be lectured about the power-of-God."

"It isn't a lecture it's the truth. You need to stop blaming God for what happened to your daddy. Things happen and God doesn't owe us any explanation. He never said life came with guarantees but He's always there to guide and comfort us when we need him."

"Okay, okay, whatever mom but what has He done for me lately that I should thank him for? Dad's death was wrong. He was a good and honest man. Knowing that the man who killed him is alive and just sitting in jail gives me the damn right to be angry with God and our corrupted so-called justice system." From the sound of Possable's voice and choking of tears her mom could tell she was upset. She also knew that it was only a matter time that God would reveal himself in her life.

"Alright baby, calm down I know you're hurt and angry but you'll going to get through this. You've always been strong enough to handle most things but only Jesus can give you peace. I love you sugar and I thank God for you and Brandon each day."

"I love you too mom and again am sorry for earlier."

"All is forgiven, sugar."

Possable smiled as a tear slide down her left cheek.

"Just live and enjoy life baby. You're too serious." They said their goodbyes with kissing sounds then hung up. Possable couldn't ask for a much better mom, but she was wrong about all that forgiveness nonsense. 8:30 a.m. was the time on her radio. Determined to get a least a few more hours of sleep she changed the ringer on the home phone to silent, picked up the sheets from off the floor, then got cozy as she drifted back to sleep.

Chapter 7

Meanwhile, things seem calm over the Summers' residence. Perhaps, they're at church pretending all is well or maybe they made up during the night. Possable was sitting outside on the terrace with Jordan reading an article in a respectable journal publication entitled "Five Signs of a Dangerous Marriage." Interestingly Rachel came to mind on part four about physical abuse. According to Rachel "life has no guarantees," so it's all right for a man to beat up on a woman. Possable knew she couldn't live with that rule, yet alone put up with a man beating her. Call her an advocate for women but she'd rather be alone. For now she had the best companion in the world, who gave her love and attention, and was a sucker for affectionate and that was Jordan. Remembering that the cell phone was still on vibration all morning, she ran inside to get it from her nightstand. There were two missed calls displayed on the screen and one new voice message. She jumped right to the message crossing her fingers that it wasn't her boss calling her to come in tomorrow for a mandatory meeting. Strangely, the message had a recording from a psychic network stating that she won a free ten minutes psychic reading to reveal what her future holds.

If it's an opportunity with sexy Officer Cruz she's all for it, but how in the heck did they get her cell number? She never understood how people could believe in those fake, lying through their teeth psychics. They usually only want you to run up your phone bill and then end up on court TV shows trying to justify why you did it. Now curiosity has crossed her mind. She decided to call and prove to herself that those phonies don't know what their talking about. She started to consider whether or not to give this free call a try. How could it hurt just this once? Finally her mind was made up she replayed the message to write down the number. She was just about to call when Jordan walked up to her with his leash in his mouth.

That familiar sign meant two things. First of all she was crazy for wanting to call and second it was time for someone's walk. They took the elevator down to the main lobby. The lobby as usually was well maintained and smelled like apple and cinnamon. Every time Jordan entered the lobby he'd stop in the same spot, smell the aroma in the air, and then move right along. Once outside, they crossed the street and headed towards the dog park. It was creativity designed by a true dog lover. First, the entrance gate had two dogs sitting side-by-side with bones in their mouths and paw prints on the ground leading to the inside of the park. Second, there is a fountain with a dog statue sitting in the middle with water coming out of its ears and mouth. Third, a huge vending machine dispensed doggy treats for only a quarter. It even had a rhyme that read, "Paws for a treat, not feet." Lastly, the park had individual training fences where owners could train or play with his or her dog one-on-one. In addition, the whole park was surrounded by many mature trees and lovely landscaping.

About fifteen minutes later, they headed back toward home; far ahead she noticed Rachel and her husband. They were dressed in church attire getting into their vehicle that was just pulled up by one of the valets. She wasn't a bit surprise seeing Rachel with shades on, but she was surprise to see the two of them laughing together while driving off. Those two were all about maintaining a happy image in public, especially the good doctor. Frankly it wasn't any of her business, but she wasn't fooled.

On the way in she went straight to her mailbox, even though she knew postal workers were off on Sundays. She hadn't checked the mail for a few days and was expecting a package. A woman who happened to notice Possable checking her mail rolled her eyes as she passed. Possable thought to herself "what's her problem?" Everything in the box was junk except a bill from the electric company.

The elevator was out-of-service for the second time this month. She marched up to the concierge desk like she was about to question one of her employees for not meeting a deadline and asked the gentlemen, "What is going on here? Twice in one month the elevator is down. Other residents and I are paying too much money each month to continue to be inconvenienced."

"Ms. Johnson, I understand your frustration and I do apologize, but apparently when the elevator breaks it's because it has gone over the capacity of weight it can support, but we have an electrician coming out to repair it tomorrow morning."

"Alright and hopefully this will be the last time. Now the only alternative is the stairs and my dog and I are not looking forward to climbing stairs to the 12th floor."

"I'm sorry for the inconvenience," replied the young concierge, who then thanked her for her understanding, and wished her a good evening.

Heavily breathing and gasping for air, Possable and Jordan finally arrived at the door and helped themselves to water to refresh and cool down. Climbing up to the 12th floor was no fun.

Noticing that the phone was on the kitchen counter; she decided to call the psychic network just for fun. A recording came on that prompted to a menu asking her to enter her cell phone number.

212-542-0114 she dialed and then the recording said, "Congrats! You have called to the right place at the right time. Ten free psychic minutes awaits you as your destiny is revealed. Thereafter you will be charged $1.99 per minute. Please hold as we transfer you to one of our live psychic readers."

"Hello this is Sandy. Is this Possable I'm speaking with?"

Yeah right, thought Possable, she wouldn't have known who I am if I hadn't entered my number at the beginning which probably generated my name from a calling list. However I'll play along, besides it's a free ten minutes away."

"Hello, are you there Possable?" she asked again.

"Yes, I'm here."

"Hello! I sense that all is well on the surface but deep down you are hurting."

A perplexed expression came across Possable's face. "What are you talking about? I'm fine."

"Yes dear, so you have convinced yourself to believe, but it's been hard to let go of a loss such as yours."

"Lady, you're good. You really are, but it's best to end this call. Besides you don't know me, lady," she said twirling a lock of her with a finger.

"I'm talking about the lost of your father!" Possable nearly dropped her cell on the floor but caught it on time and gripped it tightly.

Her voice softened when she asked, "How do you know that? You can't possibly know that."

"Sweetie your future can't be clear unless you let go of this hurt and pain."

Tears streamed down and her voice cracked, "Let go, let go. How I can? My dad will never walk me down the aisle of my wedding. He'll never be a granddaddy to his grandchildren. That part of my life was taken away from me. Do you hear me?"

"If you don't wholeheartedly, genuinely forgive the man who killed your father it will destroy your life entirely and the process has already begun. Just take a good hard look at your life and ask yourself are you truly happy?"

"Everyone keeps telling me about this let go and let God nonsense and I'm sick of it. Maybe if God will start to do His damn job maybe more people will choose to trust in Him more!"

"Your past will continue to haunt you as long as you keep it alive. You can't undo what's been done but just keep living for you and for those who love you. Your dad wants that for you and he is always with you."

Tears were now joined with sniffles. Her response was, "I can't and I won't. There's nothing in hell that will make me change my mind!"

"Then prepare yourself because more turmoil, hurts, and disappointments are heading your way and it will be an intervention from God." Upset by the statement she snapped the cell shut, threw it against the wall and wept.

Chapter 8

Monday morning a call comes through at 5:30 am. Hoping it wasn't urgent, Possable tossed and resettled in the bed. The message indicator played a jazz tune to inform that a message was left. As miserable as she felt; she was not in the mood for anyone today. Curious, she played the message on speaker and it was her best friend, Yasmin Fox.

A Canadian beauty with green eyes, long, straight black hair, naturally tan skin, and a beauty mole on top of her lip. They were best friends ever since preschool. Possable always saw Yasmin as her sister and vice versa. Their favorite song of all time is by The Supremes, "Ain't No Mountain High Enough." Yasmin was also a graduate of Penn State with a law degree. She is a big time family law attorney in Pennsylvania, who makes $300,000 dollars annually and only has been in practicing for three years. She's engaged to a man, who is also an attorney, but from Hawaii who practices employment law. They're having their home built in Honolulu, on top of a hill that overlooks the beach for only $150,000.

Apparently, her fiancée has established exceptional rapport with past clients during his 12 years of practice.

"Hello, Ms. Johnson, its Yasmin calling to let you know that J.C. Penney is having its early bird fall pre-season sale today at 7:00 a.m. and I was thinking we could go together. Call me back soon."

Shopping didn't seem like a bad idea. It definitely will help get her into a cheerier mood. Besides with autumn just around the corner, she needed to update her wardrobe with new styles. She picked up her phone and redials Yasmin's number.

"Hello, Yasmin, it's me girl, what's up?"

"Hey girl, not much just the same old stuff but a different day."

"You still up in Philadelphia?"

"Yes, and loving it."

"How's my baby, Jordan doing and your mom?"

"We all hanging in there and doing well."

"I feel I haven't seen you in years. Even though it has only been about six months, I know you're in New York because only your crazy self will wake me up this early talking about shopping."

"You know it! A trip to New York is not complete with a shopping spree. I just finished up a case yesterday and I'm flying back home to Pennsylvania latter tonight, but I had to spend some time with my girl."

"You couldn't have chosen a better time and I know you have coupons."

"Heck, yeah I got you. I'll be picking you up at 6:30; so be ready. We both know you're the one that needs an hour to get ready; especially when it comes to your looks, Ms. Vanity."

"Whatever, I'll see you in about an hour."

They both simultaneously said goodbye and hung up.

It was 6:20 a.m. and Possable was still trying to style her hair. Finally she settled for a bun with loose curls on the sides. She had on a pair of skinny jeans with a purple, V-neck long sleeve top, a pair of black sneakers, and plum lipstick to compliment the whole attire. 6:30 a.m. on the dot she grabbed her purse, a white sweater in the other hand and kissed Jordan bye. When she reached the lobby she asked the concierge to have someone from the onsite doggie daycare to pick-up Jordan.

After trying on every fall top, sweater, blouse, career pants, jeans, scarf, suit, hats, shoes, boots and selecting home décor items for their living rooms, bathrooms, bedrooms and which colors would go best for the autumn season they were exhausted.

Yasmin spent nearly four hundred dollars and Possable's total came close to almost five hundred after all discounted coupons were deducted.

"Girl, I can't even remember the last time that I shopped like this, remarked Yasmin."

"Neither can I. This was well deserved and needed," responded Possable.

They decided to eat at the food court for lunch. They both agreed on Subway sandwiches. Yasmin had the chicken teriyaki sandwich meal and Possable settled with a turkey sub meal. They choose a corner table near the display fountain that was close to the exit. While they were eating Yasmin noticed that Possable seemed kind of distant.

"What is going on in your head, girl?"

"What? Why you ask?"

"Girl, you seem distracted and so far away."

"Yeah, I'm fine just planning you know me."

"Yes I do, and I know also when something is bothering you."

"It's kind of silly. I don't even want to go into it."

"What is it, Possable? I am the last one on earth to judge you."

"Alright then, yesterday I received a weird call from a psychic network on my cell saying I won a free ten minutes psychic reading and so later in the evening I called that same number back and spoke to a lady named Sandy who apparently knew my name."

"Girl, that is weird, but maybe your information was probably on her computer screen with your cell number programmed."

"That's exactly what was thinking, Yasmin, but the strangest thing was she knew things about me. She even mentioned that I lost my dad about ten years ago."

"What? There is no way and you didn't even mention anything about your father to her initially."

"No! Of course not and besides who do you know will just voluntarily just share something personal like that with a strange, yet alone a psychic."

"Possable, what else did she said?"

"The part that really hit home was when she told me that more turmoil, disappointment, and pain are heading my way." Water filled her almond shaped eyes as tears trickled down one by one.

"That's crazy. Don't tell me you believe that nonsense. God is in control of the things that happen to us and for us."

"Like losing my father was part of God's wonderful plan for what's best?"

"Possable, I didn't mean it like that. All I'm saying is God does not owe us explanations for why life is the way it is, but He is there to help us deal with them."

"You sound just like my mother now and I don't need to be lectured especially not by you," Possable responded snappily.

"Listen, I don't want to upset you. I know I have done things in my life that I am not very proud of but I have learned from my mistakes and asked God to help me in dealing with them. Trying times are all part of God's plan as well as blessings. I am thankful to have experienced and lived through those experiences. I am a better person today for that."

"Yasmin, I am so sorry to snap at you. I just want peace in my life and happiness, is that so much to ask?"

"You deserve all that and much more, but first it all starts with forgiveness and then the peace will come." Possable was just about to comment on that when a strange number appeared on her phone.

"Hello?"

"Hi! Yes this is Dr. Perkins. I'm sorry to have disturbed you but I am calling from the Lakewood Hospital regarding Rachel Summers whose only means of contact for an emergency was your name and number. We found it in her purse along with her driver's license. She is fighting for her life and has been beaten badly. Are you able to come?"

"What! Is she?—I am on my way."

"What's going on?" questioned a worried Yasmin.

"It's my neighbor. I can't go into a whole explanation, but that call was from a Dr. Perkins saying she is in the hospital fighting for her life. Her husband beats her. Sorry but I have to go and I'll give you a call later."

"Like hell you are, I'm coming with you. This is a family crises and a woman could die because of this."

They emptied their trays and grabbed their shopping bags and ran out the exit door.

Chapter 9

Yasmin drove like a mad woman until they arrived at Lakewood Hospital. When they walked up to the information desk at the hospital lobby they were short of breath and asked for Rachel Summers' room. The man asked if were family, they both mutually answered that they were sisters.

"Sign-in and then take the elevator to the 2nd floor to room 217."

"Thanks." Convincing or not they were anxious to see Rachel.

On the 2nd floor they search desperately for room 217. A few minutes later they found it and were about to walk in quietly when suddenly a nurse startled them from behind. They jumped and turned in the direction of the voice.

"Hello ladies, is either one of you Possable?"

"Yes, I am."

"Hi, I am Nurse Davidson and Dr. Perkins got called into surgery. Thank you for coming. Mrs. Summers is not asleep yet. In about half an hour I will have to give her her medication."

"I understand we won't stay long, but is it alright to see her?"

"Yes of course, she has endured a lot of internal bleeding and has a fractured wrist. By you both being here for her it may help her pull through the night."

"Thank you, Nurse Davidson."

Possable and Yasmin held each other's hand and walked in. When Possable saw Rachel lying there helpless and broken up she placed her hands over her mouth and whispered, "Oh my God."

That was the first time since her father died that she called God's name. One of Rachel's leg and arm was supported up and bandaged. She had a busted lip; both of her eyes were swollen and connected to machines for life support. Rachel could barely see who was standing in front of her but she did recognize the voice.

"Possable I'm sorry to have bothered you, but thanks for coming I don't have anyone else and Dr. Perkins found your number in my purse and called you."

"Save your energy, don't worry about that now. This is my best friend Yasmin she was with me at the time Dr. Perkins called and she wanted to come along."

"Bless your heart, Yasmin. You barely know me but you came anyway." She tried to cry but it was too painful because of the swelling of her eyes.

Yasmin held Rachel's hand into hers and declared with tear-filled eyes, "Rachel, I am so sorry. I am here for you and I am also an attorney."

"You're the answer to my prayers."

"What do you mean, Rachel?"

"I asked God to send an angel in the form of an attorney to help me in divorcing my husband."

If Possable was an animal her ears would have popped up the instant she had heard Rachel mentioned divorce. Was Rachel considering leaving the good doctor for good?

"Yasmin, I don't have much to offer you, but I believe in my heart I can win this and I will pay you for everything. Sincerely and genuinely she asked, Please can you help me?"

"Rachel, I will take your case on one condition."

"What is that?"

"That you separate yourself from your husband immediately after the hospital releases you. Do you have family you could stay with or a friend?"

"Yes! My mother lives in Connecticut. That's where my daughter Jessica is this weekend," she replied.

"How old is your daughter?"

"She is 3 years old."

"She's just a toddler. I see the outcome of this divorce very positive for you."

Excitement filled Rachel's voice, "Do you really think I can win, Yasmin?"

"Yes, I truly do. We need to sit down when you are better to talk and plan. I am leaving my business card atop of your lovely array of flowers. I have a plane to catch back to Pennsylvania in a few hours." She kissed Rachel on the forehead and told her she will keep her in her prayers.

"Yasmin, I am thankful for you being here and wanting to help me."

"Thank me when we win. Take care and talk to you soon." She hugged Possable goodbye and give her a kiss on her cheek.

Possable looked at the wall clock and realized that Nurse Davidson would arrive to give Rachel her medicine. She sat down to comfort Rachel with words of insight and wisdom. Rachel didn't need to be reminded of her ordeal, but instead she needed a friend and a miracle to get through what may be her last night.

Chapter 10

Bright and early Possable awoke and did her morning regime. She reluctantly prepared to return to work after a long and trying Labor Day weekend. She styled her hair while reminiscencing about the events that took place over the weekend and shook her head. Jordan was stretched out on the bedroom floor. The Weather Channel was on and calling for somewhat fall-like temperatures around sixty degrees. She opened her huge walk in closet to decide what to wear.

"My plum skirt and a purple blazer will do just fine," she thought to herself. She noticed that it was already 6:45 a.m. on her radio. If she expected to be ahead of traffic into the city she had 15 minutes to get dressed and be out the door. Time management was a pet peeve of hers.

At 8:00 a.m. everyone said their typical good morning greetings. The main office topic was about what they did over the weekend and complaining about returning back to work. Allen, the security guard for the main building of KG Marketing greeted

Possable with his warm usual friendly smile. Reaching her department Possable smiled and greeted everyone to include her secretary, Angela, as well as her manager Mr. Rio.

Possable entered her office and exhaled. She anxiously picked up the phone and dialed the number to Lakewood Hospital. A gentleman at the front desk answered.

"Good morning, Lakewood Hospital can I help you?"

"Good morning, can you transfer me to room number 217?"

"Certainly, please hold."

Possable started making tapping noises with her fingernails while listening to music in the background when suddenly Angela barged into her office with files in her hands and startled Possable which caused her to disconnect the call.

"I am so sorry, Ms. Johnson. I hope that was not a client."

Possable breathed heavily and folded her arms together and replied, "Angela, just next time knock on the door to let me know it's you. Now what can I do for you?"

"Yes, Mr. Rio had ask to me give you these files in order for you to sign them."

"Alright, leave them on my desk. Please, close the door behind you. I don't want to be disturbed for at least an hour."

"Yes, Ms. Johnson," Angela answered with a shaky voice.

"Angela would you relax? You aren't in any kind of trouble. Okay?"

"Alright, thanks. I will see to it that you don't get disturbed."

"Thanks and by the way you're doing a fantastic job. I couldn't do most of my work without you. And do me a favor stop calling me Ms. Johnson."

A big smile came across Angela's face. She replied, "Thanks so much Ms. Johns—I mean Possable."

"You're welcome." Angela slowly closed the door behind as she exited.

* * *

Angela was a divorced single mom for two years now raising two children. A 10-year-old daughter named Alana and a 7-year-old boy named Jeremiah. Her ex-husband is a respected real estate agent in the New York area. Without Possable's job offer and for having completed her Bachelor's in Marketing from NYU, Angela would not have been granted by the judge (whom Angela believed was bought off) full custody of the children. In addition, Angela was only awarded $800 dollars a month in child support and no spousal alimony.

*   *   *

Possable grabbed the phone once more and redialed Lakewood Hospital.

"Good Morning, Lakewood Hospital how can I help you?"

"Hi, can I be transferred to room 217, please?"

"Was that room 217, you said?"

"Yes, that is correct."

"I'm sorry but that room is not available."

Possable's raised the volume in her voice when she asked, "What do you mean it's not available?"

"It is no longer occupied."

"What does that mean exactly?"

"Listen, I don't know who you are and what you want, but this here is a hospital and we have the right to protect the patient's privacy."

"I understand that. However, can you tell me if the patient has been transferred to another room?"

"No, I can't! Quit your interrogating unless you got an emergency." Then the line went dead.

Frustrated she slammed her fist unto her desk. She was debating if she should call back and tell that so-called receptionist to go to hell. Nibbling on a fingernail she decided to redial. Perhaps remind that jerk of a person that she was just there yesterday. She deeply sighed and dialed each digit with a pulse in between. The plan was to plea concern and act pleasant in hopes to find out about Rachel.

"Good morning this is Lakewood Hospital. This is Cruz speaking can I help you?"

Could this be the same Cruz like in Officer Cruz that was at her residence over the weekend? But why would he answer the phone; she had to think fast. Hopefully, her voice didn't sound familiar.

"Hello?" he repeated once more.

"Hi, I'm Yasmin. I was at the hospital last night visiting my sister Rachel. I wanted to know if you could transfer me to her room 217, please.

"Room 217, that room is unoccupied at this time."

"Unoccupied? Is she alright?"

"If your sister was there last night she is not there now."

"Oh! Did they transfer her to another room?"

"Lady, if you are that concerned about your sister why don't you give her call?"

"She doesn't own a phone, yet alone a cell phone. Besides, her crazy husband beats on her." Possable just revealed her identity if this was the same officer Cruz from a few days ago. She crossed her fingers hoping it wasn't.

"Did you say that your sister's husband beats her? I just had a similar case like that over the weekend that involved a so-called noble doctor and his wife."

Possable bit down on her lips and replied, "Isn't that funny?"

"I know and your voice sounds so familiar too."

Possable gulped and chose to ignore the statement and boldly replied, "Did they transfer my sister to another room or not? "

"Hold on for a second?"

Impatiently Possable held on. It wasn't until five minutes that officer Cruz picked up again.

"I spoke with Nurse Davidson and she informed me that *your* sister made it through the night and was released early this morning."

With a breath of relief she said, "Thank goodness."

Cruz inquisitively asked, "By the way aren't you that lady—?" There was only a dial tone at the other end of the line before he could complete his question.

Chapter 11

Two Months Later.

Thanksgiving was just three weeks away and Possable's neighbor Rachel was separated from her abusive husband. According to her attorney, she could file a contestable divorce mentioning the abuse in the marriage and the court would grant her a divorce and full custody of her daughter in less than a month. Rachel was determined to do whatever it took to put an end to the drama in her life. A few weeks later the divorce was granted and Dr. Summers was ordered by the judge to pay Rachel both spousal and child support in the amount of $2,500 a month for the next three years. In addition, Dr. Summers had to attend for one year anger and alcoholic counseling, in order to not have his medical license revoked. Rachel was also ordered to attend at least six months of domestic violence counseling sessions as well.

Possable's apartment was festively decorated for the fall. Her house purchase would be finalized next month and she could declare herself an official homeowner before Christmas. Everything was going well as planned; she even sponsored a child overseas. This year for Thanksgiving she decided to spend it with her mother and brother in Pennsylvania. Life was definitely good, even more so because her best friend Yasmin would be getting married in December and she would be the maid of honor. After the wedding, Yasmin and her new husband planned to relocate to Hawaii in the spring.

During the evening as Possable was watching "America's Got Talent" on the screen a special report from the news station interrupted the show and her cell phone rang at the same time and an unfamiliar number appeared. Reluctantly she answered it.

"Hello is this Possable?" This is Nicholas D'Angelo, Yasmin's fiancé.

Though surprised and confused at the same time, Possable responded.

"Hi, Nicholas it is good to hear from you. I have heard so many things about you. Yasmin keeps going on about how wonderful you are. I'm sorry—but what can I do for you?"

"I'm not sure how to tell you this, but it's about Yasmin."

"I just spoke with her last night and she was scheduled for a flight to Chicago this morning for a case today."

Nicholas voice weakened as tears started to drop one by one. "She's gone."

"Gone?! What do you mean, *gone*?"

"Her plane crashed and it killed a few passengers and Yasmin was one of them. It's been on the news and radio stations all afternoon. Haven't you heard?"

Possable burst out in tears and fell on her knees dropping her cell phone along with it. She quickly grabbed the remote that had fallen from her sofa to increase the volume on the television. There on the news the unreal was true. A photo of Yasmin flashed on the screen. There she was her sweet and dear Yasmin; her one and only best friend since preschool. The person that was a sister to her that was always there to make sense of everything. She was always fun and daring and didn't care what anyone thought of her.

Yasmin introduced Possable to the world of fashion, music, and entertainment. They shared intimate secrets about all their relationships together. They both grew up in the same neighborhood and during the holidays both families would come together to cook a lovely meal and make Christmas special and meaningful.

Brandon would chase both of them with his pet lizard and drive both their moms crazy. Possable kept repeating the phrase, "Oh, God," as tears fell harder and harder. She cried and cried and the only one there to comfort her was Jordan. In fact, she held unto him so tightly until she cried herself to sleep.

Chapter 12

On Tuesday at 10:00 a.m. family and friends gathered at New Hope and Praise Fellowship Church in Pennsylvania to say farewell to their beloved Yasmin. Her broken-hearted mother, Carol was there along with Yasmin's fiancé, Nicholas and all Yasmin's kinfolks and few friends from over the years. Two of which Possable recognized but didn't feel like engaging in conversation. Yolanda, Possable's mom was present, and Brandon.

Reverend Mitchell Carter began with a short interlude describing who Yasmin was and how she lived her life. A half hour later the choir sang one of Yasmin's favorite gospel songs

I Love the Lord. A young soloist by the name of Carmen led the choir with a voice of an angel. Throughout the congregation there were cries of pain and hurt. Some folks had their heads bowed and others closed their eyes allowing the music and the lyrics to console them.

One lady even uncontrollably threw herself onto the floor and shouted, "Jesus! Please hear my cry."

When the choir concluded their song, Carol took the stage. She appeared strong and confident, but was crying from the inside. In one hand she held the Bible and asked the congregation to turn to Psalm 23. From the pews everyone picked up the Bible and turned to Psalm 23 and followed along as Carol read the scripture out loud. She spoke about her daughter with so much love and adoration. She mentioned all the little amazing things she used to do as a child. Also on how determined Yasmin was whenever she set her mind to accomplish something. Carol shared of Yasmin's favorite pastimes and collectibles.

At the very end of the speech, the church displayed photographs of Yasmin's life from childhood to adulthood, including her graduation from Penn State University. Carol shed tears as she stepped down from the podium. Yolanda comforted Carol by rubbing her shoulders as she too was in tears.

Shortly after, Possable addressed the mourners with a poem she had written to recite in honor of her friend. It was carefully composed with thought and insight. She shut her eyes, took a deep breath, then exhaled and began to speak from her heart and not from the paper in front of her. The congregation felt the deep emotion in her voice and pure sincerity behind her words.

Yasmin you have been my best friend since preschool

You were always the one that was fun-filled and cool

I remember your first crush, Paul, in our six grade math class

Remember how hard we studied together so that we could pass

We convinced our moms to let us go to school dances

And a few times we cut classes to go to the mall as we took our chances

I remember those snowy winter days when we would go out to play

And how Brandon would chase us in his sleigh

And remember those nights when our parents were at work and we would talk for hours on the phone

Until one of them or Brandon came home

And then there were those special times

When our families would eat and celebrate together

Especially around Christmas- your favorite holiday

*With a fireplace, and a lovely, decorated
    tree, and your cousin Heather
You were a joy and blessing to everyone
We always talked about having our own
    children
You wanted your first to be a son
And his name would be Joseph because
    "Joseph and his Brothers" was your
    favorite story from the Bible
Although you are not here in flesh
I wanted to let you know
That I love you and miss you
Our fondest memories and moments
Will always be in my heart
Neither space nor time could put us apart
You are in a place of peace and love
May your legacy and sweetness be with us
    always even from up above.*

Possable choked on the last words because tears of sadness. The piece of paper that was filled with words was now saturated, but Possable didn't care. All she wanted was for her best friend to know and listen to her as she poured out her heart to her. She took the wet paper and stepped down from the pulpit and sat between her mother and Brandon in the front row.

Nicholas took the stand next and shared how he and Yasmin met and the plans they had made together. It was at a jazz club in Philly. He knew in his heart from the start that they were destined to be together. He described the various qualities he loved most about her such as: her pretty smile, how she'd style her hair, her exhilarating scent, her refreshing personality. He even described how she was when she wasn't in her career mode. She enjoyed nature and all its splendor and beauty; including how children were drawn to her like magnets. Her favorite flower combinations were yellow tulips and red carnations. He ended by commenting on the one thing that linked them together: a spiritual bond. Nicholas didn't shed any tears on the surface, but Possable knew that like most men he will in his own time and way.

Rev. Carter again took the podium and led the congregation into a short and insightful prayer. The sermon title was on <u>Hurts</u>. He then asked the congregation to repeat the phrase, "The past does not determine my future."He then asked them to turn in the Bibles to several illustrations that related to this topic. He spoke of Abraham, Moses, and Joseph and how God used their situations to show His power and might. People in the crowd shouted their yes's, amen's, Jesus', glory's, and hallelujah's. Rev. Carter touched on how even in our own lives and situations that if God is trusted He can work it all out. Throughout all our sorrows, disappointments, and guilt He is there ready and able to forgive, but we must humble ourselves. We must not give in to our situations from a negative standpoint but from God's perspective. We can be so quick to blame God for everything that happens to us. However, the goods and bad in life is what makes us stronger and become better individuals. Thankfully He sent His one and only son, Jesus to suffer and save us. So yes, God knows and understands our every need and pain. He wants to deliver us and comfort us through them, but only if you surrender it all to Him."

Rev. Carter then asked, "Didn't God say I will never leave you nor forsake you?" What happened yesterday, last week, last month, last year, 10 years ago, should not stop you from trusting and loving God because only He alone can give you peace and make you whole. God never said life will be easy or fair but he did promise to be with you when those dark clouds come your way and bring illness, confusion, and even death. Brothers and sisters in Christ let us not lose heart or hope in the things that bestow us here on earth, but let us rejoice and look forward to the promises of God. Knowing that one day we, also, will be with our Father in heaven forever."

He ended with amen and asked if anyone who is in search for peace-of-mind and true happiness to come forth and accept Christ Jesus into their hearts. He emphasized the importance that today is promised, not tomorrow.

A couple in tears walked up together hand-in-hand. They shared that the illness of their daughter had created a wedge in their marriage. They were tired of the negative poison that caused constant bickering and blame and they were planning to separate.

Rev. Carter first and foremost thanked God for sending them today and prayed for them as well as the congregation that God will give them peace and direct their lives and heart according to His will. He also asked that God touch the life of the couples' daughter and banish her illness by the hands of The Great Physician that can come only from above. Thanking God that not even Satan himself can try to break them apart, but with the Lord's grace he failed. He told the couple afterwards that it is well and that all will be well and to go with peace from this day forth together in unison as a family.

There was another lost soul among the crowd that the reverend could feel was hurting deeply but concealing it on the surface. This lost spirit longed for peace from the past.

"Come forth lost soul," he called out "and receive that inner peace and joy that only Jesus can give you. No material possessions or person can restore for you or fill that void in your heart."

Possable felt as though he was speaking directly to her, but she ignored his call. Perhaps, he was referring to another person. Once more he called out for that one soul to come forth and receive their peace and blessing. Possable felt uncomfortable, but at the same time convinced herself that Rev. Carter was not referring to her. Her heart started beating rapidly as her pulse races because she wanted desperately to go forth, but it was almost like something was holding her back. Suddenly, Rev. Carter asked everyone to please take their seats and announced that the service would end after one last song from the choir.

Everyone took a seat as Rev. Carter stepped down from the podium. He made eye contact with Possable. She saw the look of disappointed in his eyes before taking a seat. It was as almost he knew *that she was that lost soul.*

At the burial site family and friends shouted in agony and wept. Carol and Yolanda stood beside each other holding a red carnation and Nicholas, Brandon, and Possable all stood together. All waiting for Rev. Carter to gave the signal to place flowers on top of Yasmin's casket. He then once again led everyone in prayer and asked God to be with the family and loved ones. Carol, Nicholas, and Possable all speakers at the service each had a special keepsake to place on top of the casket. Carol had brought Yasmin's childhood blanket and Nicholas placed a wood statue of a deer with a picture of him and Yasmin. It was the time when they participated in a cause that was raising funds against child neglect and abuse. Finally, Possable placed a heart shaped locket that had a photo of the two of them when they were in third grade. The inscription read, "Best Friends Forever."

Yasmin's casket covered with flowers, roses, and sentimental memories and keepsakes was lowered into the ground little by little everyone watched, cried, and silently said goodbye. When it was over everyone hugged and shared their condolences with Carol and departed graciously. Carol, Yolanda, Nicholas, Brandon, and Possable were the only ones that remained as they watched the cars drive away, one after the next.

Suddenly a trickle of water turned into drizzle as they walked to their cars together in gloom. Carol briefly talked with Nicholas encouraging him to move on with his life, although it would be hard initially. Nicholas agreed and Carol thanked him for being a part of her little girl's life and adding to her happiness. They hugged compassionately and he gave Carol a kiss on her check.

He hugged the others. When he came to Possable, he kissed her hands and said, "Yasmin couldn't ask for a much better friend. Your words spoken at church were inspirational and moving."

Possable kissed him on the cheek and thanked him for just loving her best friend and wished him well. Nicholas got into his champagne colored Nissan Pathfinder and drove away. The rain came down harder as they all entered Brandon's blue Infiniti SUV and decided to go over Carol's home for the remainder of the day. As Brandon drove, Possable remembered when Yasmin told her once that when she died she wanted it to rain at her funeral. Could it be possible that God himself was saddened? If so, then He must have opened the doors of heaven to bring forth His tears in the form of rain to express His pain.

Chapter 13

At Carol's house silence fell in between them all. A house that was once filled with love and laughter was lost in words of expression and nothing could undo or reverse what had been done. Noticing a picture of what looked like Mrs. Fox when she was younger, Brandon broke the ice when he commented, "Mrs. Fox is that you? You were a sexy mama."

"Yes, Brandon that is me. That's an old picture. I was about 22 years old there and much skinner too. I guess all those years of cooking caught up to with me." Cooking was one of Mrs. Fox favorite thing to do. She offered to serve up a hot bowl of homemade chicken soup.

Possable walked into the spacious country-styled kitchen to offer assistance. Mrs. Fox told her that she was fine.

Possable then went outside where she could be alone to cry. The view from the deck was breathtaking. She looked at the magnificent trail of Evergreen trees on opposite sides and it leading straight to the mountains great and high. Mrs. Fox's house was in the mountain side of Pennsylvania, because just like Yasmin, she loved nature too. She remembered how at age thirteen she and Yasmin and two other girlfriends from school decided to go camping for the first time in the backyard. Everything was fun and exciting until it got pitch dark. They heard all kinds of noises from creeping noisy bugs, rustling of bushes, and even Yasmin's overhearing of a wolf howling in the night. They all ran out of their tents and banged on Mrs. Fox's back door to be rescued. A smile came across Possable's face after that passing thought. She fought back the new tears that were about ready to flow when she noticed Brandon sitting on one of the deck chairs crying.

She sat down next to him and reached out and squeezed his hand. Her little baby brother was hurting. She extended her arm to embrace him to let him know that they were all going to get through this together. She excused herself to give him space to be alone in order to reflect.

Inside the pleasant aroma from Mrs. Fox's soup filled the room. Yolanda was setting the table with silverware and dishes. Brandon returned a little regrouped, but still deeply torn. After hands were washed, Yolanda led them into prayer. While enjoying the soup, they all exchanged sincere and agreeable smiles that it was delicious. During the meal Yolanda insisted that Carol gives her the recipe for the soup. Carol politely changed the subject to announce that she has decided to sell her house.

"Oh, why Mrs. Fox? This house holds a lot of precious memories and history. This is like a second home to me." said Possable.

"I know sweetie, but the plan was to do it next year after Yasmin's move and Yasmin didn't like my decision either but she understood it. I will be retiring next month and have decided to move back home to Canada with my sister."

"Carol you worked so hard to keep this home even after your husband passed. It will be so sad to see you give it up, but I respect your decision," replied Yolanda.

"Thanks and believe me it was a tough choice to make, but I appreciate all your support and love, especially now more than ever. Enough about that subject, before I forget, Possable in Yasmin's room there is something on her bed for you. According to Yasmin's will, she wanted you to have it. Go check it out."

Possable placed her empty bowl in the kitchen sink and walked upstairs. When she reached the final step, she stood in front of Yasmin's closed bedroom door. She stood right there and cried softly finding it difficult to turn the doorknob. She so wished that when she opened the door that Yasmin will be standing there in flesh and bones, but that would not be the case. She finally found the strength and courage to turn the knob.

The walls were still painted in shades of purple and pink displaying all her awards. Her five piece contemporary bedroom furniture from Ashley's Furniture was neatly arranged. The theme of the décor was nature and all its beauty along with it. A tall bookcase in a corner stood with all her favorite collections of books from various writers, including a series of *The Babysitter's Club.* There was also CD's and DVD's from various singers and actors. Next to the bookcase Yasmin's computer desk was there with all the necessary school materials and extra storage bins. The comforter on the bed had a picture of a deer family in the woods among trees beside a brook with a mountain in the background. She had matching window curtains, pillow shams and sheets to go along with it. Possable then walked in Yasmin's bathroom and it was creatively decorated with a wolf theme with a shower curtain, bath mat, toilet seat cover and even the 3-set towel matched. When Possable returned back to the bed she noticed a diary and a scrapbook. The scrapbook read, "Best Friends Moments." She sat on the bed and began to cry when all of a sudden Mrs. Fox walked in.

Carol walked over and sat next to Possable, "Honey, it is difficult now, but with time we heal. I do miss Yasmin like crazy, but I know that she went to be with the Lord and that someday I also will see her again in heaven. You got to believe that too."

"I know, Mrs. Fox, but it's so hard."

"Yes, it is. Losing someone near and dear to us is, but we've got to move forward and remember the good things we shared with that person while they were here on earth."

Possable rested her head on Mrs. Fox's shoulder and wept. "Possable, look at me and stop shedding those tears from your pretty eyes. Though I have lost both my husband and my daughter in less than a few years apart, I should be angry with God. But instead I am at peace. Remember when you and Yasmin were little girls and we used to read stories about Jesus and how he told his disciples that he will go into heaven and prepare a place for them and all who believed and lived a righteous life He will come back for?"

"Yes, I do."

"So when someone dies and leaves this earth it is our Father calling them home to be with Him eternally. Initially there is sadness and tears, but at the same time you know in your heart that they are in a better place. A place where there is no more suffering, hurt, pain, or disappointment and that is why I am at peace."

"You're right, Mrs. Fox and a wise woman."

"Don't you know you are and will always be like a daughter to me? I am here for you always as long as God will allow. Feel free to call me whenever or even write to me when I move. Just hold on to those sweet, precious memories that you and Yasmin shared because she's alive in your mind and heart. I love you, baby and so do Jesus." Carol kissed Possable on the forehand and hugged her affectionately.

"I love you too, Mrs. Fox."

They both turned to the first page of Yasmin's scrapbook which was an old picture of the Foxes' when they first move into their house and the community. Next they came across another photo of when Mr. Fox, Mrs. Fox, Yolanda, Brandon, Possable, and even Yasmin had a family cookout during the Fourth of July holiday.

"You see Possable even back then Yasmin knew she had a best friend for life."

They smiled and shared a few laughs as they turned each page in the scrapbook one by one and reminisced.

Chapter 14

Early the next morning Possable decided to see Rev. Carter. Although she was still grieving the loss of her best friend she felt compelled to somehow open up. She felt a need to talk to someone about what she was going through on the inside. She sat in her parked car for a few minutes, debating whether to enter the church or just forget about the whole idea.

She managed to find the courage and walked up the church ramp and entered the building. Other than Yasmin's funeral service, she hadn't been back to church ever since her father died. From the view inside nothing has changed from the signs, symbols, paintings and ceiling fixtures. When she turned the corner to go towards Rev. Carter's office, she noticed his office was the only door opened with the lights on. Anxiety was beginning to build in her chest and she was having second thoughts. She slowed her pace, took a long, deep breath before popping her head into the door. Amazingly, it was empty. However, a posted sign with an orange background read that he could be found in the sanctuary. Perhaps, he was in the sanctuary studying his Bible or praying. It was a good excuse for Possable to get the heck out of there before he spotted her. Besides he may not want to be disturbed anyway. She was just about to walk out the church doors when a familiar voice suddenly called her name.

"Possable, Possable Johnson."

She turned back around to associate the voice with the face. It was Rev. Carter. He was shaking a teenage boy's hand, telling him that he wanted to see more of him participating in the Youth Ministry program. The young boy nodded his head and smiled all the way out the church doors.

"Possable, it is good to see you and I know why you have come."

What the heck was that suppose to mean thought Possable to herself. "Do you really?"

"I believe you know also and God has already revealed the reason to me."

There was no way of disguising anything when it came to Rev. Carter. He was truly a man of faith and disciple of God. Possable smiling follows him to the sanctuary. They sat together in one of the front pews. Rev. Carter then asked for Possable's hands as he led them in prayer.

"Father God, I want to thank you for bringing Possable into your house today. Help her to express her thoughts and emotions freely and openly. Father you are the only One who is able to deliver and lift up any burdens, doubts, fears, or pains in her heart and life. Bring healing and comfort to your child right this moment. Finally, Father I ask that you may use me to counsel her into reaching that ultimate level of her destiny. In Your Precious Name I pray, Amen."

Possable smiled gently. She looked up at the cross and read the words that were beneath the cross: *I am the way, the truth, and the light.* She sighed.

"Rev. Carter I want to start by saying I was ashamed yesterday during Yasmin's funeral service to come forth. I was the one you were referring too."

"I know, Possable."

"I felt you knew because when you stepped down from the podium, you gave me a look that caused me to feel guilty."

"I know that as well." They laughed together.

"I never could keep anything away from both you and my parents."

After mentioning parents, a feeling of sadness came over her and she bowed her head looking down at her hands.

"Possable, are you alright?"

She thought about the question and was about to answer yes to it, but then instantly realized who she was trying to fool.

"No, I miss my father terribly. My life has not been the same without him around. I have been hurting for ten years now and have shut God out of my life entirely because He is to blame."

"I understand the heartache and pain one feels after losing a loved one, but I don't understand why you think you shut God out of your life. You see Possable, God was there that day at the school with the incident involving that young man who was upset about being kicked off the football team."

"How was God there? My father was murdered. Instantly, his life was taken from him by one of his own students. So how could you sit there and tell me that God was there?" She folded her arms and deeply sighed, flushed irritability.

"GOD WAS THERE!" You could have been the one lying on the floor dead. Your breath, life, and future would and could have been taken from you, but your dad chose to sacrifice his life instead of yours.

God does not bring destruction and turmoil into our lives. He gives all His children free will and with that comes making a choice whether to live your life godly or ungodly. Don't you see? God is the reason you are here in front of me today. Ten years later. He is the reason why you graduated from college, have a successful career, and the reason you wake up each and every day. So don't you tell me that God have not been there for you?"

Once more guilt and dismay filled the mind and heart of Possable because she never viewed her pain and hurt in the way that Rev. Carter just described it. Her eyes filled with water as she tried to refrain from crying. The Reverend took pity on her and held her in his arms allowing her to cry on his shoulder. A few minutes later, Possable regained her composure and sat upright; drying her last tears with the handkerchief that he gave her.

"Rev. Carter you're right about all the things you said about God, but—I mean it's so hard to let go of this pain of my father. I miss and love him so much. I don't want to keep living my life anger at God. I just don't know what to do."

"It's alright to miss your dad and perhaps wish that he was here, but you have to know and believe that he is and has always been with you all these years. He is in your heart and thoughts every day and moment. Don't let go of the memories you shared with him."

"How can I get through this? Please help me."

"Is that young man still in jail?"

"Do you mean the one—?"

"Yes! Is he?"

"Yes, but why?"

"Well, my dear Possable the first step to the healing process is having a breakthrough. And the next step has to do with forgiveness."

"**D**on't tell me you mean—?"

"You know exactly what I mean."

She dropped her face into her hands and breathed into them. She straightened up, made eye contact with the reverend and nodded her head.

"Possable, you are about to embark on a journey to not only heal but also renew your strength and embrace faith. Imagine blessings will overflow and so many that you would not be able to count. You see, you were once a prisoner of unforgiveness, but soon you will be set free."

"I like the sound of that, but can you come with me Rev. Carter?"

"When do you want to go?"

"Tomorrow is my last day here. I have to get back to New York. How about tomorrow, is that good for you?"

"Tomorrow is never promised Possable, how about today?"

"You mean right now?"

"Yes, right now. Let's go!"

Chapter 15

"You are now entering Pennsylvania State Prison" read the sign at the entrance. Two armed muscular guards stood outside the gated restricted area as Possable and Rev. Carter drove up to them. One guard had a bald head and wore shades. He demanded to know who they were and what they wanted. Possable frowned and thought to herself how unnecessary his attitude was and wondered who he was trying to impress.

Rev. Carter paid no mind to his rudeness and responded, "Yes, hello I'm Rev. Carter and we're here to see Jimmy Nelson."

"Did you call in advance to be put on the visitor list?"

"We weren't aware that we needed to call, can you pardon us just this once and we will be sure to do so next time."

"Look, man, or whatever you may call yourself. My job is to secure the entrance of this gate and grant access to only certain individuals at a time."

"It's Rev. Carter and I understand you have a job to do. So do I, but the only difference is mine is constant whether personally or professionally."

They both smiled.

"You got that part right Rev. Carter. My shift ends in another two hours. I tell you what, I'll make an exception this time, but next time you have to call this number on this card and be put on the visitor's list. We have to conduct a thorough vehicle inspection without you both in the car. It's protocol for all visitors."

They both exited the car, stood on the curb as they watched the bald-headed guardsman inspect the car. Ten minutes later he returned and told them everything checked out okay.

"You guys are free to go" as he waved a hand signal for the guards sitting in the booth on the other side of the gate

"I appreciate it. Have a blessed day."

"You're good, Rev. Carter," mentioned Possable.

"No Possable, God is good. Besides you got to know how to talk to people."

They spotted seven armed guards in total as they neared the visitor's parking lot. They parked and walked up to the visitor's building together. The reverend carried along his Bible in one hand. The glass door was double-sided so that anyone on the inside could see who was standing outside prior to granting access. They heard a woman's voice over the intercom.

"Can I help you?"

"Hello, we are here to visit the inmate Jimmy."

"Jimmy? We have a few Jimmies here. What's his last name?"

"Nelson, Jimmy Nelson."

"Hold on a minute."

Five minutes later Possable was getting a little impatient and that was the moment when they were finally buzzed in.

The same voice heard earlier was a woman to their surprise when they approached the security desk. She was a heavy-set woman who had a 1960's hairdo, chapped lips, huge frog-like eyes, and a double chin. A few inches away from her desk were a metal detector.

"Hello I'm Possable Johnson and this is Rev. Car—."

"Yea, yea, yeah, I needs to see ya'lls photo ID's and for ya'll to remove all them jewelry, keys, metals of any sort, and place it here in this plastic bin and for one at a time to go through the metal detector."

Possable rolled her eyes. Apparently that woman had a serious attitude problem that needed to be adjusted along with a fashion makeover. Reverend Carter paid her no mind for he was here for a mission only. Possable did as the lady instructed walking through the metal detector with Rev. Carter following.

"Ya'll need to take the elevator to level three. After ya'll gets ya'll things from *off my plastic bin.*"

Ignoring the rude demand, they gathered their items and took the elevator. Upon arriving at their designated floor, Possable had a combination of animosity and nervousness and Rev. Carter could sense it.

"Possable you can do this and I am here to help."

"I know just a little nervous."

"Just remember God is here at this moment to give you guidance and deliverance."

"Thank you for being here with me."

"I just thank God for bringing us here together today."

They walked towards the sign reading "VISTORS" and found two seats. A short, robust guard from afar noticed them and walked towards their direction to assist them.

Chapter 15

"Hello, you are here to see who?" implied the guardsman.

"Brother Jimmy," replied Rev. Carter?

"Do you mean Jimmy the inmate?"

"Yes, thank you."

"I'll be back. Kindly wait. By any chance, are you family of his?"

"No! I mean no," responded Possable

"No, sir we are here to pay a visit that is all. Why do you ask?" inquired the reverend.

"Because he has not had a single visitor for the past ten years, I can't imagine what that feels like."

Rev. Carter felt pity for Jimmy and others in his place that never had visitors, including never knowing the love and peace that can only be found through the Lord Jesus Christ.

Possable was watching TV when she noticed ahead a guy who resembled Jimmy somewhat. He looked rough but matured in an unusual way. His height hid the short guard who followed behind him. They stopped and the guard pointed where Jimmy should go. Suddenly the inmate's whole facial expression changed sour. His was disgusted and displeased to see Possable there. He turned and started walking back to the direction of his cell. The short guard demanded that Jimmy turn back in the opposite direction towards his visitors. Jimmy refused and began an altercation between the two of them. That's when a taller, bulkier guard with a dragon tattoo on his arm interrupted them.

Rev. Carter stood and walked toward them. "What seems to be the problem?"

"Jimmy doesn't want to see you guys," answered the short guardsman.

One of Rev. Carter's many gifts was his wise way of talking in any situation. "I can understand why Brother Jimmy might feel that way. He probably has not had a single visitor since he's been here. Now here comes some preacher man and this woman from his past to pass judgment on him for what he committed. I don't blame him at all."

The guards exchanged a perplexed look and then turned their focus back on Jimmy.

"So, are you saying you do not want to speak with him Reverend?" inquired the taller guard.

"I am going to leave that up to Brother Jimmy. And if he decides to I am only asking for thirty minutes of his time."

"Well, Jimmy what you—?"

"I can speak for myself," interrupted Jimmy as he stared at the reverend studying him intently. "Just thirty minutes, huh? And no disrespect to you, but you is again?"

"Rev. Carter."

"Thirty minutes is cool. I can handle that."

"Alright so it's settled. Gentlemen I thank you, please excuse us."

Possable watched the whole thing from a distance and was speechless. As they approached the bench closer her heart started to beat faster, her throat felt dry and scratchy and her palms felt sweaty. She went into the restroom. Inside, Possable took deep breathes and splashed water on her face to help cool her nerves. She let out one deep sigh, checked her appearance in the mirror once more and exited.

Rev. Carter and Jimmy were sitting on the bench patiently waiting for her return. She sat down next to the reverend and stubbornly refused to greet the murderer sitting across from them. Jimmy just smirked. Rev. Carter sensed the tension so he initiated the conversation.

"Brother Jimmy, as I stated a few minutes ago that we are not here to pass judgment on you. We are here hoping to restore peace. Both Possable and I had a meeting this morning that allowed her to have a breakthrough regarding the situation that transpired about ten years ago with her father,

Cooper Johnson. She wants to let go of her anger and be able to forgive you."

"Yeah, so what because she had a breakthrough you expect me to congratulate her and give her a medal?"

"No, Jimmy not at all. That is not what I am saying. I am asking that both you and she can forgive each other."

"Forgive her for what? That I will be spending the rest of my life or maybe I should say death here. I admitted and still admit what I did was wrong, but as I tried to tell the court and family it was an accident. I never meant for things to escalate to murder. I could never do anything like that. I was angry about being kicked off the football team. My plan was to scare Mr. Johnson to the point where he would reconsider his decision."

"I know we humans don't consider the consequences of our actions until it is too late or sometimes someone gets—."

Possable interrupted. "You took from me my hero, my father. A man that was loved by his family and in turn a family that loved him so much. You left my mom a widow alone to raise us without at the beginning a job to struggle and learn to fend without the security of having my father around.

All you can say to me is you never meant to cost a dear and innocent man's life and it was an accident. Man, you are a punk and will always remain one. All because you didn't like the fact you were kicked off the stupid team and look where your stupid plan landed you. I am glad your ass is going to rot in this jailhouse."

"Yo! Whatever, Possable! Besides, you always had the support of family and what did I have going for me-just sports. I had no one. When my mama died when I was nine years my Pops abandoned my brother and me. We bounced from one foster home to another. You don't know anything. Don't think your ass is better than me. I needed so desperately to be put back on that football team; so that I can play in college. My plan with God's grace was to work hard enough to be blessed and worthy to play professionally someday. I wanted to give my baby brother a brighter future, so that he can become a better person than my dad. Have an opportunity to make something positive out of his life. I can't undo what has been done!"

"You're damn right about that! You can't," responded Possable. A part of her also felt saddened by his story. Suddenly tears came down one-by-one.

Rev. Carter allowed her and him to continue expressing emotions because it was the beginning for healing and forgiveness on both ends. He knew he would be the one to conclude the conversation.

For some reason, Jimmy felt her hurt and hung his head low. Rev. Carter knew that God had touched each of them at the heart.

Possable and Jimmy's eyes filled with tears as they looked at each other and collectively said, "I'm sorry."

"Ladies first, so go ahead."

"I have been living the last ten years of my life in angry, hatred, and unforgiveness. I have also blamed God too and been disobedient to His will. I just lost my best friend, Yasmin, yesterday and although I miss her like crazy, but I know she is at peace. I also feel that God took her away from me to show me that He is in control regardless. I just want peace in my life and want to ask you to forgive me for hating you from afar in my heart and thoughts all these years. I can only imagine what you went through as a child and had I not come today I would have never learned the reasoning behind your actions. I judged you so quickly and I'm so sorry," she wept as Rev. Carter handed her a tissue.

"I do forgive you, Possable. Please forgive me and believe me when I say I never ever meant to kill your father and cause you and your family so much pain. I deserve to be paying for what I did and God will punish me even in hell for what I did and I am truly sorry for everything. That is probably why my brother and grandparents have not come to visit me. They're ashamed of me. I wish both God and you could forgive me and someday my family."

"I do forgive you Jimmy for everything with all my heart and soul."

"Son, God has already forgiven you, but it starts with you forgiving yourself," remarked Reverend Carter.

"How do I do that, Rev.?"

"First, you need to confess and accept Jesus as your personal Savior and Lord." He opened up his Bible and turned to John 3:16 and showed Jimmy the words, *"for God loved the world he sent his only begotten Son that whosoever believeth in Him shall not perish, but has everlasting life."*

"Are you saying that all will be forgiven just by asking Christ to come into my heart?"

"Yes! But those are not my words. They are the powerful words of truth. If you desire to be set free, then open your heart to Jesus. He will transform you inside out and all past sins mistakes will be forgiven."

"Is it that simple?"

"It starts with a confession and belief in Christ. I know it's hard and seems impossible to think that one simple thing can make God forgive you, but belief and you will see."

Suddenly, the short guard appeared from nowhere and said that 30 minutes had passed.

"Give us more time," replied Jimmy.

"Your time is up, *NOW*!" shouted the guard as he grabbed Jimmy by his arm.

Angrily Jimmy replied, "No! I said to give us more time."

Abruptly, three guards with sticks charged towards Jimmy as Rev. Carter interrupted, "That won't be necessary. We just need ten more minutes and we will be done."

The short guard rolled his eyes and replied with authority, "Ten minutes! And I'll be clocking you." Jimmy let out a deep sigh.

"Just brush it off son; you won't get sympathy from anyone in here. Just let it go believe me I know."

"You sound like you did some time yourself, Rev."

"I did in the past until someone noticed and cared for me enough to bring me to Jesus and then I rededicated my life to God that same day."

"I never knew that," Possable replied.

"I am not perfect you know. I once had a past too. We all have."

"Reverend Carter I want you to pray for me. Like you, I want to rededicate my life to God also and receive his forgiveness and blessings."

"Why don't we all pray together?"

They all held hands and despite who was looking bowed their heads and closed their eyes.

"Father God once more we are gathered in your presence asking you to bless this day and uplift our hearts and minds. Father God I want to ask you to first and foremost forgive Jimmy for his sins and his past, for he was a man lost, but he is found. Lord please hear and receive his confession and re-enter in his life and transform it with your love, power, and spirit. Today both Possable and Jimmy have begun the process of healing by forgiving both each. Father God, hear and accept Jimmy's confession to you."

Nervously Jimmy spoke, "Lord please takes me as I am and change me. I ask that you forgive me for all that I have done wrong in my life, including murdering a man, a husband, and a father. I just want you to know that I am so sorry for the pain I have caused. I thank you God for sending Rev. Carter here today in order to bring me to the light and truth. Also, thanks for allowing Possable to forgive me. I ask for your peace, forgiveness, and love today."

Rev. Carter continued, "Yes! Jesus can you bless this day and make it holy. I also want to ask you Lord to give me strength and guidance for I have decided to start a prison ministry at the church to reach out to other brother inmates so they can come to know you like Jimmy did today. I ask all these things to today in your precious name, Amen."

When they opened their eyes Jimmy was in tears and not embarrassed to show it. Rev. Carter embraced him as they stood and he placed a cross necklace on his chest. He kissed him on his forehead. "It is well and God is with you."

Possable and Jimmy also hugged each other knowing all will be well from this day forth. Rev. Carter handed Jimmy a copy of the Holy Bible as an early Christmas gift and told him to read it daily and reflect on the words. He also gave him his business card with the church address.

"Feel free to write or call me whenever you have the chance. Can you help me in reaching out to other inmates?"

Jimmy felt honored and smiled agreeably. Shortly after the short guard returned and noticed standing in front of him was a different Jimmy from the one earlier. He recognized the look and knew Jimmy was at peace within himself and God. Yes, indeed Jimmy was a changed man. He felt it deep inside his spirit and heart. Saying one last goodbye, Rev. Carter and Possable watched Jimmy leave through a rear door.

Possable had only one day left before returning to New York but had to say a final goodbye to Mrs. Fox.

Chapter 16

Possable awoke at 7:30 a.m. made her usually coffee and drove to Mrs. Fox's house. On her way there, she called her mom from her cell phone to share her experience with Jimmy the day before.

"Hi! You have reached Yolanda. Sorry to have missed your call, but kindly leave a message and have a blessed day."

She's probably still asleep, Possable said out loud. "Hey, mom it's me. I'm on my way to see Mrs. Fox. I'll give you a call later on. Love you."

After climbing what seemed like a relentless mountain trail, she finally arrived at Mrs. Fox's driveway and parked the car. She had on red jeans with a matching red coat as walked up to the front door. Just when she was about to knock, Mrs. Fox opened the door and greeted her with a warm and pleasant smile.

"Good morning, angel," she said while extending her arms to embrace her.

"Good morning, Mrs. Fox. I came to spend some time with you."

"It is always a pleasure seeing you, but don't you have to head back to New York?"

"Yes, I do, but my flight leaves later this evening at 6 p.m."

"Ok, so how are you dear? You look radiant, like a burden has been lifted of your shoulders." See invited her to join her outside on the enclosed deck.

"Oh, it has. I feel more at peace now."

"Peace is a wonderful word and it comes in many forms and shapes. Why do you say you're at peace now?

"Yesterday, I went down to the prison with Rev. Carter. That's where Jimmy is incarcerated. The three of us sat down and talked. It wasn't easy for me, Mrs. Fox. So many angry words were exchanged. In fact, you see I have been angry for so long."

"I think you mean angry with God all these years and blame him as well."

"Yes, Mrs. Fox, but how did you know that?"

"Angel, I haven't been around all these years just to get old. It's called wisdom. It has taught me a lot over the years through times of joy, disappointments, pain, hurt, and even loss. Also, that God is in control-despite everything that happens to us. Be it good or bad or ugly, He still loves us, strengthens us, and most important blesses us."

Possable's eyes filled with water as Mrs. Fox's words touched her spirit.

"Baby, you've reached a point in life—although tough and painful—where you have forgiven the young man that wronged your father and found peace. And now with your newfound peace comes a new beginning for you to prosper in all areas of your life."

"That's what I have been searching for all these years, and perhaps in some way God prepared me to be right where I am at this moment in my life."

"Yes, He did and don't ever stop trusting in the Lord. I am so glad you stopped by today Possable. Oh—silly me. I forgot to give you this the other day." It was a small diary.

"What is this?"

"It's Yasmin's diary. She wanted you to have it in. Keep it, embrace it, and remember all that you both shared together."

"Thank you, I will cherish it forever," she said with a little sadness.

"You okay, Possable?"

"Yeah, I just miss Yasmin."

"I know, I know, me too everyday," she said gracefully."

"I wish she was here now, you know."

"So do I."

They hugged knowing that it will be their last before saying goodbye.

Mrs. Fox held Possable's hand in hers as they walked towards the front door. They embraced once more and Possable gave Mrs. Fox a kiss on each cheek and said she loved her.

"Oh! I almost forgot your Christmas gifts, Possable. Wait here a minute."

"Mrs. Fox you shouldn't-."

"I found it! Here it is," she shouted from the living room.

"Mrs. Fox you are too generous." She appeared with three beautifully wrapped gifts. The largest in gold, the next in size was silver, and the smallest in red. Mrs. Fox opened a large gift bag to place all the gifts inside. She also handed Possable a card.

"Mrs. Fox—," Possable said graciously.

"I'm not listening. It's the holidays and also a time for giving. I want you to know that I am always here for you. I love you very much and that I am very proud of too."

Tears streamed down Possable's face. "I love you too Mrs. Fox and thank you so much for everything, especially for my best friend Yasmin."

"You will always be a daughter to me. I want you to also keep in touch with me. You have my new address for Canada. Take care sweetie and remain blessed."

"Yes! You keep in touch also."

"You know I will honey. Besides, what if you or Brandon decides to get married?" Possable smiled.

Mrs. Fox watched as Possable back out of the driveway. She waved until Possable's car was out of sight.

Chapter 17

Early Sunday morning, a U-Haul truck pulled into Mrs. Fox's driveway and parked in front of her colonial house. She greeted all four men and offered them coffee, hot chocolate, and bagels in the kitchen. About ten minutes later they start to load the furniture and boxes into the truck. One of the men, Gary, made a comment.

"Why are you selling you're beautiful home, Mrs. Fox?"

"I am moving back to Canada, to be with my family. Also, I have lost my only daughter a few days ago and my husband two years ago."

"Sorry to hear about your losses. Have any potential buyers come along yet?"

"Yes, plenty have. In fact I closed yesterday evening."

"Well, that's good."

"Why do you ask Gary?

"Well, homeownership is my goal for next year."

"That's good for you and I'll keep you in my prayers too."

"Thanks! I guess I better get back to work. We have a busy and long day ahead of us."

*   *   *

Possable waited at the airport for her flight, which would depart in about an hour. She was reading an inspirational book that Rev. Carter gave her. She was on the topic about relationships where it talks about the different types, and embracing them all. Moreover, how our thoughts, feelings, and actions can universally attract the right or wrong kind of people to us. Just when the book was getting so intense her cell phone rang.

"Hello."

"Yes, Hello Ms. Johnson. This is Andrew Wentworth."

"Hey, how are you?"

"I am superb. I should be asking you the same question, with the funeral and everything."

"I'm holding up. Each day it's a little easier."

"Ok, we'll I'll get straight to the reason for my call. I have some great news."

"You do?"

"You will be able to move into your own house before Christmas, Ms. Johnson. How does that sound?"

"Wow!—that's *this weekend*, that's wonderful news. I thought we were looking after the first of the year. What happened?"

"That was the original plan, but things happen for a reason."

"I hear you. I am so thrilled. I have so much to do. There's packing, scheduling leave at work, then there's the office 10th year Christmas party this Thursday and—."

"I'm sorry to interrupt Ms. Johnson, but I have a client that just walked in. Could I give you a call back later?"

"I'm on my way back to New York. I am so, so, happy. You really made my day, and I think they just announced my flight number. Yes, definitely give me a ring back later this evening or at work tomorrow. Thank you so much."

"No problem, Possable. How late will you be—?"

The line went dead just before Andrew could ask his question. He just smiled to himself and hung up the phone.

Chapter 17

Once on the plane Possable ordered an Apple Martini to help calm and relax her. Flying was not her forte. She found herself easily distracted while attempting to read as other passengers were boarding the plane. She noticed one gentleman in military attire sitting to the right of her reading the same book.

"Ladies and gentlemen, this is Captain Miller speaking. We'll be taking off in five minutes. I ask that you remain in your seats and fasten on your seat belts. Please refrain from using the bathroom until we are in the air. Our flight attendants are here to help meet your needs or concerns that you may have. Thanks for your cooperation."

When Possable arrived home it was 2:00 p.m. She was scheduled to pick-up Jordan from the pet sitter at 6:00 p.m. But first, she was going to enjoy a few hours to herself. First, she contacted the concierge at the front desk and asked to be transferred to in-room dining to place an order. Fifteen minutes later a server arrived with a turkey club sandwich with lettuce, tomatoes, and red onions and a side order of seasoned fries and a coke. Later in the evening Possable read Yasmin's diary while enjoying a glass of white wine soaking in the tub. Laughter filled the room as she remembered the funny experiences they shared.

Chapter 18

The official KG Marketing 10th annual Christmas party had finally arrived on Thursday December 21st. Angela planned the whole thing for weeks. The office was decorated with a bold and lively seven foot pine tree with all the traditional bells and ornaments of all kinds of styles, shapes, and colors. An illuminated star sat gracefully on top of the tree. Each desk had a holiday animal figurine in colors of red, green, silver or blue.

Possable's desk had a crystal angel and the base was highlighted in gold and it read, 'faith, hope, and love. The greatest of these is Love. 1 Corinthians 13:13.' She sat and admired the angel thinking to her self all these years it was God who loved and never gave up on her, despite the fact she was angry with Him. A commotion outside her office interrupted her wandering thoughts. She raced outside and to her surprise she saw a person dressed in a Santa Claus suit carrying a sack filled with gifts. Everyone was filled with excitement as they temporarily transferred into their childhood state of mind, eyes filled with wonderment, and chanting "Santa, Santa, is here." Everyone turned to one another whispering and wondering what Santa has brought. The man inside the Santa suit was nonetheless than Mr. Rio. He asked for everyone's attention to make some announcements.

"Happy Holidays to all. How are you all doing?"

"Good, fine, okay" were the various responses.

"Alright let's try again! This time with more jolly in your voices. Again, how is everyone doing today?"

"Wonderful, great," one guy even shouted "glad to here!"

"That's much better HO, HO, and HO! I bet you all are wondering why on earth I am dressed as Santa. I'll tell you why because it's our 10th annual Christmas party and I wanted to do something different in a special weird way. Another reason is because I'm the boss."

Laughter filled the room. "Most importantly this is the event I look forward to each year. I'm pretty sure you've notice that this year holiday party is taking place during the afternoon versus past years during the evening. One main reason for that is that the weather center is calling for three or four inches of snow tonight. I'm sorry I live up in the mountains and I am not going to be bold to try to drive in it."

Possable thought to herself that this is the weekend she'll be moving into her very own house.

"I have some announcements to make before we get into the holiday spirit. First announcement I think everyone is going to love. We will be closed from Friday, December 22nd through Wednesday, December 26th."

Everyone was jumping up and down, hugging one another, and yelling.

"Okay, okay, I'm excited too, but there's more. Everyone's getting a bonus this year whether you just joined our organization or you've been with us for ages, regardless of title. Finally, I need Possable to come up and join me in announcing our new Marketing Manager, a newly created position that was approved by our CEO."

Possable smiled and walked gracefully because she knew who was going to receive the recognition.

"Thank you, Possable for joining me. Please put your hands together for a wonderful congrats to Angela Bello as our new Marketing Manager."

Angela put her hand over her mouth in surprise. Applauses surrounded the whole office. She accepted her accolade in tears and expressed her heartfelt gratitude.

"I just want to first thank God, if it wasn't for Him this will not be possible. I am so grateful for this moment. I will continue to provide exemplary service even in my new position. I also look forward to continue to grow both professionally and personally."

"Angela if you can now follow me to my office. I have something for you," said Mr. Rio.

Still in amazement Angela followed behind Mr. Rio. As they entered the office, he offered Angela a seat. Then he opened his top drawer and pulled out a white sealed envelope stamped with the KG Marketing's logo and handed it to Angela.

"Angela in this letter you will find your job description, your new pay increase, and what additional benefits and bonuses you will receive in your new position."

"Thanks, Mr. Rio. Do I need to open it now?"

"Of course not, open it when you get home tonight and be sure to sign and date the bottom of the letter and give it to me when we return after the Holiday break."

"I'll be sure to do that, Mr. Rio."

"Yes, and I believe you will very pleased, especially with the generous pay increase." He gestured.

He then led Angela to her new office space that was next door to Possable's. The window floor to ceiling window was huge with a view of the city. Angela was overjoyed with the breathtaking view and the comfortable spacious new office. The executive, leather chair looked perfect with the layout of the office. Taking a letter opener from the supplies lined up on her desk, she said a short prayer prior to opening the envelope. This is what it read:

Dear Ms. Angela Bello:

We are so pleased with the wonderful job performance you have continued to provide for the last three years. You are an important individual to the success and growth of the company. Your job is a vital part of our organization, which is why we would like to offer you the newly created position, as the Marketing Manager. This opportunity was taken into extreme consideration prior to offering it to you. We will like for you to continue your career development with us as KG Marketing continues to move forward. Please review the following:

Job Description

Overseeing a team of seven Marketing Executives and sometimes working closely with the Director of Marketing to innovate, integrate, and present business solutions that upholds the integrity of KG Marketing. We strive to provide stellar professionalism. We will continue to build rapport with all our business accounts and relationships through quality customer service and innovative product knowledge.

Compensation

Your new position starts with an annual salary of $80,000 per year. In addition, you will receive quarterly bonuses of 5% of total revenue sold by the marketing executive team. **Benefits:** You are now eligible to have your 401k matched by KG Marketing 50%. Effective next year January your dental care coverage will be fully covered by the company.

<u>Effective Date</u>

The position is available to you immediately upon receipt of this signed acceptance letter.

Respectfully,
Alejandro Case
Human Resources Administrator
KG Marketing, Inc.

A huge, satisfied smile came across Angela's face. She shut the door and did a victory dance, leaping for joy as she shouted out, "Thank You Jesus, thank you Father God."

She quickly composed herself, looked once more at the layout of the office especially the stunning view and returned to join the rest of the crew of KG Marketing.

She returned just in time because the carters arrived. There were three staff members setting up in the lounge area. There were platters of sandwiches, mini- wraps, bowls of assorted fruit, garden fresh salads, varieties of pasta sides, grilled chicken strips, exquisite cheese and crackers, assorted breads, spinach dip, macaroni and cheese, mash potatoes, beverages and trays filled with baked desserts. Mouth-watering chocolate swirl brownies, moist carrot cake, cheesecake, and Boston crème pie. Minutes later, the caterers announced that everything was ready and for all to come eat and be merry.

Suddenly *Have a Holly Jolly Christmas* started to play as people lined up to enjoy the delicious food. Possable started to sing-a-long and tapped her feet to the beat, a few others joined her. Some employees shared their holiday plans while eating. The Christmas spirit and magic was definitely alive in the KG Marketing office fiesta that day.

Chapter 19

It was four days until Christmas and the evening news predicted three inches of snow, but the movers promised Possable it would not delay her big day. Bright and early the movers arrived on time. They had to have the truck to another address by 4 p.m. They came into the building with dollies to load and transport furniture and boxes items. Three hours later they were ready to hit the road. Possable was excited. She led the movers in her Infiniti FX SUV to her new residence. Finally she was moving into a place of her own, with no more late night music playing and no more sirens from cops or ambulance drivers. Thankfully, she didn't have to complain about any resident above her because she was on the top floor. She had to admit she did love and would miss that view of the skyscrapers and glowing lights over top the Brooklyn Bridge. The commute from *Steady Seasons* to her new house was approximately 20 miles and that would be an extra 30 minute for her in the morning to get to get to work. But it is all going to be worthwhile. For starters, Jordan would have a huge backyard to run around and play. She already had plans to adopt another puppy at the animal shelter soon. Now that Jordan is two, it will be nice for him have a little brother to play with. The house was surrounded by nature because it was inside the vicinity of a serene park-like setting. The community block was shared with eight other homes and was just about 30 minutes away from the outskirts of the city limits.

Arriving at Serene Pine Community outside each red brick lovely two-story home were two-car garages, trees, and shrubs. They arrived at 348 Serene Drive. A curved walkway lead to the front door, all built on an acre and half of land with 2400 square feet of living space. The inside looked like a model inside that you would find listed on a broker's website or a publication of home listings. There were a total of three bedrooms, two full baths and a half bathroom. The entrance into the foyer area had hardwood flooring, a carpeted family room with a wood burning fireplace openings to the stairway, ceramic tile floors in the spacious cherry kitchen with granite countertops. The breakfast area sported a bar and had French doors that overlooked the large deck to the rear of the home which was perfect for outdoor entertaining. The best part is the nearest neighbor was about 100 yards away separated by a white fence. The breakfast area opened to the living room with a loft. On the first floor there was an office and a half bath in the hallway near the coat closet. The basement had a family room with a beautiful stone fireplace. Double entry doors lead to a relaxing sunroom where Possable could enjoy the view of the lovely landscaping and fish pond. A sliding door opened to an outside brick patio area where a portable fire pit created an ambience and warmth with either charcoal or firewood. There was also a laundry center downstairs in the basement. The second floor featured two bedrooms including a deluxe master bedroom suite with a cathedral ceiling, an electric fireplace with a remote control, two huge walk-in closets, and inside the private bathroom featured an oval window right atop of the corner whirlpool tub, a large stand-up shower, and double bowl vanity with raised cabinets.

Nearby a brook and more woods were there to enjoy, along with the wildlife that can be seen from time-to-time. The community was vastly diverse, with a few children playing in the street, a few dogs walking alongside their pet owners, and surprisingly quiet at night, at least from what Possable's real estate agent, Andrew had told her.

The mover's gave Possable compliments of her new home then started to work right away in unloading the truck. Possable guided them to where she wanted the sectional in the living room and the dinette set in the dining room rather than in the breakfast area in the kitchen. She had her eyes set on another kitchen set that will be perfect for the breakfast area. While two of the guys were working on the lower-level arranging the living room and the office furniture as Possable instructed, she asked the other two workers to follow her upstairs so they can be instructed on how she wanted the bedroom furniture placed.

Possable had a six-piece, Queen size traditional cherry Maplewood finished style bedroom furniture included a head and foot board, one night stand with three drawers, a five chest of drawers, a dresser and mirror, and a beige oriental style area rug. The master bedroom had two double paned windows on opposite ends that would be perfect for putting up curtains and the bed would go dead in the center. The view from the windows showed a forest of trees and the endless sky. By 2:30 p.m. despite the fact that all the heavy furniture and items were assembled, arranged, and put in place the house still seemed empty. Between cardboard boxes upstairs and downstairs, she still had personal items that had to be unpacked and stored away. The basement and the extra bedroom upstairs both still had to be fully furnished, but all in time. Suddenly, the doorbell rang and it was a delivery person with 2 large pizzas, an order of breadsticks, and a 6-pack of coke. After lunch the movers expressed their gratitude, but they had to hurry to their next moving address.

During the course of the weekend, items in the boxes were stored away or put out for home décor throughout the house. Jordan happily followed Possable everywhere in the house, sniffing and familiarizing his new environment and probably wondering how soon and when they would return to their other home. By Sunday afternoon Possable received friendly visits from the neighbors in the community with house warming gifts such as gift cards, flowers, and desserts. She accepted all the gifts whole-heartedly as she introduced herself and Jordan. One of the neighbors suggested that her dog, Mitch and Jordan have a play date very soon. Possable agreed, but she would like to get settled first, perhaps sometime in January after the holidays.

Later that evening Possable took Jordan for a walk to the park area in the neighborhood where there were a few other pet owners outdoors. The area was well-lit at night and the design was in a circle surrounded by Evergreen trees and regular trees. There was a fenced-in small lake and in the middle was a statue of a family of deer that illuminated colors of a rainbow. There were also two benches, one in green and the other in brown. Nearby was also a sign that asked pet walkers to pick-up after their pets and to use the convenient pooch bags and waste basket. A nature trail led to more trees in the serene woods.

Shortly after returning home, Jordan made himself very comfortable near the fireplace in the family room. Possable thought to herself that the warmth of the fireplace was an exceptional idea since it was a bit nippy outside. She gathered firewood and started a fire. Within minutes the area felt as comforting as a warm blanket. Amazingly, Jordan fell asleep from watching the sparks of the fire. Possable's heart melted just watching him sleeping so sound and peaceful. While in the middle of decorating the Christmas tree, her cell rings and it was her mom. "Hello mom."

"Hey baby, how are you doing? Are you settling into the new place?"

"Yes, it's very lovely and peaceful around here. Not to mention that the neighbors are friendly and know how to make a newcomer feel very welcomed.

"Great! How did you enjoy working with Andrew?

"He's been so great and professionally from start to finish.

"Wonderful, you know us real estate agents are passionate about what we do and it shows in our personalities. Do you have any plans for the holidays perhaps a party to attend or dinner with a special someone?"

"No, the only party I'd attended was at our 10th annual Holiday office party."

"That's right. Angela was given a promotion of some sort right?"

"Yup and she blissfully accepted it with a new corner office too."

"I am so thrilled for her she deserves it. She's sharp with lots of innovation. Well I wish we all could get together this year for the holidays, but remember Eric planned a romantic holiday getaway up in the Pocono Mountains in Pennsylvania. I am so excited. We'll have a lovely two-room log cabin with a built-in stone wood burning fireplace and not to mention the view of nature will be breathtaking. We will be leaving in a few hours and I wanted to call my children and wish them both a lovely and safe Merry Christmas filled with lovely surprises."

"Merry Christmas to you too mama and say hi to Eric for me. By the way, mama do you still believe in miracles?"

"Yes, baby. God has been so good to us throughout this year. Just take you for an example. You are different person inside and out. You confronted the man who took papa's life and genuinely and whole-heartedly forgave him which brought upon peace in your heart and spirit. You have a wonderful career in marketing and making very good money, you were blessed to move into your very own home before the holidays, but watch and see that God has much more in store for you still. Who knows maybe your future husband-to-be may be closer than you realize."

"Thanks mama you always had a way of explaining things in a spiritual way. I love you mama very much. Thanks for being in my life."

"Girl, you got me in tears. Remember I love you too baby and am here for you always. Even, if it's just to talk. You and Brandon are my greatest treasures and gifts beyond measure that I could ask for. See, even if we are not together for the holidays in person, we are in spirit."

"Perhaps, next year we can all get together for the holidays at my house. What do you think?"

"I'm going to hold you to that." They laughed.

"I mean it mom. I'd like you and Eric, Brandon and his girlfriend Angelina to all come over next year for the holidays. It will be fun."

"It will be wonderful and special. Let's try to make it happen."

"Well alright, it sounds like Eric is calling you that dinner's ready. I love his Italian dishes. You are lucky to be dating a chef."

"No, it's more like a blessing. Believe me when I say your time is nearing for happiness with a wonderful man too. I love you very much, but I got to go."

"Love you too mama. Bye and have fun."

Chapter 20

The clock chimed at the stroke of 8:00 a.m. with the sounds of children laughing and yelling outside the windowpanes. In the same vicinity of the community, a few dogs barked. Jordan joined right in trying to keep in rhythm with the other dogs. At last, Christmas Day had arrived bringing with it that morning a beautiful snowfall. Possable stood up from her bed and put on her cotton terry plush pink robe and scurried downstairs with Jordan trailing behind her to the kitchen to make some tea. While waiting for the kettle to come to a boiling hiss, she made her way to the half bath across from the den to fresh up herself. Pouring some dog food into Jordan's bowl; she decided to drink tea from her one and only traditional holiday polar bear mug that she had received from Yasmin a few years back. While pouring the hot water into the mug that had a bag of peppermint tea, she realized this will the first year that she would not receive a friendly Merry Christmas call from her best friend on the other end of the telephone. Dwelling on the thought, her cell phone rang. She quickly sipped a taste of the tea before answering with a hello.

"Hey baby. It's Mrs. Fox, Merry Christmas, how are you?"

"Oh. My goodness! Mrs. Fox, Merry Christmas to you, this is a wonderful surprise."

"I was calling to wish you a Merry Christmas."

Possable's tears trickled down her cheeks. "I miss you so much. How is everything in Canada?"

"Cold and wet, we had a snowstorm last night, but the view is indescribably beautiful. This is my kind of holiday season. I am here with my sister, Hope, and her dog, Dash."

"That's wonderful. It's so good to hear from you. Sounds like things are going well."

"Yes, but enough about me, are you still at the apartment or have you settled into a home for yourself, yet? And how is my little guy, Jordan?"

"Yes, I moved into my own house just Friday, and Jordan is good. He seems to be adjusting rather easily. I like it here. It's quiet and I know how you would love the view of the mountains here."

"It sounds like you are enjoying the change of scenery too. There is nothing like peace of mind. I bet the neighbors and community is comfortable too. So, have you opened the gifts I gave you, yet?"

"No, I have not had a chance yet. Today is only the first day of Christmas."

"Are you waiting for New Year's Day? I remember when you and Yasmin couldn't wait for Christmas morning to arrive to open your presents under the tree," They chuckled.

"Just getting up and into my morning, I am planning on doing so today. Mrs. Fox, I'm so very glad to hear from you. It's funny because I was just thinking about Yasmin and how this will be the first holiday without her."

"I had my moment of reflection just last night when we had a small dinner party here at the house. I miss her terribly, but I know and believe in my heart, Yasmin would want us to live each moment of our lives with love and joy. I try to remember the good things. That's what gets me through each day."

"Yeah, you're absolutely right. Yasmin was the type of person who didn't like or wanted those whom she loved to feel unloved or unhappy. She had a beautiful spirit and she left a beautiful legacy in the hearts of the lives of children she touched too."

"That was my baby and always will be. You are my baby too and I love you, but listen we will talk soon again. I need to get ready for church. Remember the true meaning of Christmas is in giving and not receiving. When we give openly of our time, selves, and love; it always finds a way to return goodness and joy back into our lives."

"I'll remember. I think I will visit a children's hospital center and spend some quality time with the children. I feel called and moved to do that today."

"That's God calling you. Who knows maybe you will find a special someone or something just for yourself."

Possable was tickled by Mrs. Fox's comment.

"Anything is possible. Listen I love you, Mrs. Fox. Merry Christmas and we will talk soon and take care. Bye."

Possable arrived at Children Angel Foster Clinic in a taxi. She bought two gigantic holiday bags filled with toys and books for the children. The cab driver helped her to carry and drag one of the heavy and hefty bags to the pediatric center.

Upon arriving, Possable spoke with a Ms. Rosslyn, who is the Head Nurse of the pediatric center. At the entrance of the pediatric care center, a woman dressed in a teddy bear shrug with her hair pulled back into a bun and bangs flowing evenly across her forehead welcomed her.

"Merry Christmas! Hi, you must be Possable. We spoke over the phone. I am Rosslyn."

"Hi Rosslyn, it's good to meet you. Yes, I am Possable. Thank you so much for permitting me to come by and visit the children on such short notice. I know things like this are usually planned in advance."

"Typically they are, but its Christmas. Besides, we have visitors all the time especially around this time of year. Bringing gifts and sharing stories with the children. Last year a volunteer dressed up as Santa for us, it was very entertaining for the children. I see you brought bags of goodies, it is safe to assume that it is for the children."

"Of course! I bought a variety of toys, books and clothing items for various age groups."

"That is very generous of you. It must have been so much time and money spent in doing this. I sorry you went through all this trouble."

"It was no trouble at all. I felt moved to do this. Strangely so, I was touched by an angel."

"Oh, yes! Here at Children Angels Foster Clinic I have seen a lot of miraculous things happened; in fact, by angels in disguise like you all the time."

A child caught spying was asked by Nurse Rosslyn to tell the other children to come out and choose gifts they favored. One by one the children came out shouting with glee as their eyes lighted up with excitement. Possable assisted Nurse Rosslyn and a few other staff members in passing out gifts to the children. Then the children gathered in a circle for storytelling time with a cup of milk and few cookies. The time shared with the children opening gifts and playing with them was absolutely wonderful.

Putting back on her coat Possable remarked, "Merry Christmas everyone. Take care."

"Merry Christmas to you, Ms. Johnson," replied the children and staff.

Walking out the clinic to signal a taxi, she remembered one of her favorite Spanish restaurants, "Bonita's" just a few blocks up the street corner. Curious to see if they were even open, she decided to walk. To her amazing discovery, Bonita's was opened, but was scheduled to close at 2 p.m. Overjoyed to see a familiar face when she entered. She walked right up to the counter and smiled excitedly, "Hola, Senior Reyes, como tu estas?"

"Senorita, Possable. It's you. How are you? It's been a long time."

"I know! I think it has been maybe twelve years."

"Hey Dios! Mucho tiempo. How's your family?"

"Everyone is good. My brother is now a middle school teacher."

"That's good. You look very beautiful."

"Gracias! I didn't know you worked here."

"Yes! As a matter of fact, I own it. I have been here two anos."

"Wow! I think the last time I was here was three years ago."

"Do you still like arroz y pollo con ensalada like old times?"

"Si, me gusta mucho," she replied with a smile.

"Well, one order of arroz y pollo coming up. I wish you came earlier we had a nice holiday bunch that ended about twenty minutes ago."

Just when she is getting ready to reply a man showed up with firewood and to Possable's amazement she couldn't believe it.

"Hola papa," the man greeted.

"Hola, Alex! Hijo. Guess who's here?" Mr. Reyes said.

Possable walked towards him. "I thought that was you. How have you been all these years?"

She was standing in front of a six feet, slim but muscular-build, very good-looking guy.

With a very huge smile on his face he replied, "Possable hey. How are you? I didn't expect to find you here on Christmas Day." Looking at the expression on his face; he was in awe with how totally beautiful she looked. The first thought that came to his mind was it had to be fate or some intervention on God's behalf. Alex was very sexy. He had a mocha latte complexion and he was half African and half Puerto-Rican with chestnut brown eyes and a goatee. He and Possable used to live in the same neighborhood together, but when his mom died, he and his dad moved back to Puerto Rico when he was 15 years old. However, it was in his senior year at Penn State University he saw Possable again. Call it love when he saw Possable in her sophomore year. At the time Alex was dating Erica, but immediately upon seeing Possable, his heart and interests were directly set on her. All that he knew was that she was all grown up and utterly more beautiful than he ever imagined. He had hoped that one day he would see her again. If so, he was not letting her go because it had to be fate. Unfortunately, right before he was going to break up with Erica, to his dismay she informed him that she was pregnant and that the child was his. He didn't challenge what she said because they had been together a few times and their dating was exclusive, at least he thought so. As a result, his course of action then was to do the right thing, marry Erica, and take care of his responsibility as a father should in supporting his family. After graduating from Penn State with a Bachelor's in Accounting, he landed a fantastic job as a contractor for the government. The opportunity could not have came at a more opportune time because it gave him the stability he needed to support his family; in addition, to great benefits and a solid career path.

"I am great. How is Erica?"

"She's in Florida spending the holidays with her family."

"Do you mind if I ask you another question?"

"Go ahead."

"Why aren't you in Florida with her?"

"We broke up. Things didn't work out between us. I found out that my daughter was never mine, but by some guy she had a one night stand with back in college who dumped her after telling him that she was pregnant with his child. Surprisingly, he also got drafted into the NBA. I was so hurt; I felt betrayed and used. Over the years I grew to love both Erica and my daughter very much. All that time I thought she was mine. We separated and a year later divorced."

"I'm sorry to hear that."

"Thanks, but moving back here to New York at age 35 was a fresh start. I am close to family and they have been so supportive. Furthermore, I just got offered a new job opportunity working at a law firm as an Accountant."

"That's great news. When do you start and who is the company?"

"I start the day after New Year's Day. The company is Liriano & Associates, LLP."

"I am very familiar with them. In fact, we did an interview with the CEO a while back." "Are you still working with Greater Marketing?"

"No, in fact I am now a director with KG Marketing and actually I am on holiday leave from now until the day after New Year's Day as well. I can't believe you still remember Greater Marketing."

"There are lots I remember about you Ms. Director. I'm sure you have big plans for the remaining of your holiday."

"Actually I don't have any."

"Really?"

"You seem surprised?"

"I am. What about your family?"

Mr. Reyes purposely interrupted them, handling Possable her meal to go. He kissed her gently on her cheeks and told her to come back again soon. While Possable's back was turned, Mr. Reyes gestured for Alex to ask Possable out. Mr. Reyes then blurts out, "Alex lock up the restaurant for me. I'm on my way to Tia Maria's casa."

"Okay papa! By the way, Feliz Navidad!"

"Feliz Navidad, Alex and Possable."

"Feliz Navidad to you Sr. Reyes," waving goodbye to him as he exits the restaurant.

Possable took that as her cue, grabbing her food and started walking towards the door, not really wanting to.

"Hey Possable, what are you doing tomorrow night?"

"I don't have any plans as of yet, why?"

"I was wondering if you would like to go out, maybe go see a movie. Besides it will give us a chance to catch up some more."

"Yeah, that's cool. How should I dress?"

"Well, I am sure anything you wear will look good."

Possable giggled bashfully and smiled. "Where do you want to meet?"

"I can pick you up, but only if you're comfortable with that?"

"I am." Possable wrote down her address for Alex on a napkin.

"I can pick you up at 7:00."

"That sounds good."

"By the way, you still have the dog? What's his name again?"

"Jordan?"

"No, it was a more common name. I think his name was Chance."

"Oh, Chance. He was my parent's beagle. He passed away about five years ago.

"Sorry to hear that."

"Yeah, he was a horrendous loss to us, we all took it pretty hard, but thankfully I have another great pal waiting for me at the house."

"You bought a house that's great. What type of dog? Let me walk you to your car."

"He's a chocolate Labrador Retriever. Wait a minute; I almost forget I took a taxi here."

"Where's your car?"

"Parked in my garage at home; I went gift shopping for the children at Children Angels Foster Clinic and dropped off a bunch of toys, books, games, and other stuff."

Alex smiled because Possable had always had a good heart and she could possibly be the woman he can spend his life with.

"You have always been special and I like that about you."

"You are so silly."

"It was so sweet of you to take the time to bring joy and cheer to the children at the foster center and that alone make you remarkable. You are totally amazing. Now, please allow me to drive you home because I will feel better knowing you got home safely. Besides with it being Christmas and the snow accumulating there's no telling when the next taxi will arrive."

For some strange reason Possable felt safe with Alex and believed his intentions were sincere. Perhaps, he could be the one for her. During the ride to Possable's house they talked more about their families and life after college. They arrive at Possable's front door which was the only one in the neighborhood that had a gold and white winter wreath.

"Thanks for the ride, I appreciate it."

"Sure and I am so looking forward to seeing you again tomorrow."

Possable didn't comment. She just smiled. "You said around seven, right?"

"Yes, I'll see you then. Have a good night."

"You too and thanks again. Be careful driving." She realized she sounded like a concern girlfriend. She waved goodbye as he pulled out of her driveway.

Once inside, Possable greeted and kissed Jordan on his head then hurried to over the tree to open gifts. First, she opened one for Jordan. It was a rubber toy. Almost forgetting the one she received from Ms. Hill next door, she let's Jordan enjoy unwrapping it. Right in the middle of opening her gifts, Possable saw the frustration on Jordan's face because he wasn't breaking through the green box as fast as he wanted. Possable shook her head and smiled and thought Jordan is still in little ways a puppy. Once the green box was opened, she was surprised to find a little stuffed, brown gingerbread man.

"How cute, Jordan. Just for you. Here boy come get it."

Jordan leaped up from his comfortable spot just as excited as he could be because he was anticipating the fun of the new toy. He gently took the toy from Possable's hand and suddenly it made a squeaky sound. Possable giggled as she watched Jordan scurried to a corner to enjoy his gift. Just watching Jordan you could tell he was enjoying himself because one minute he would roll over onto his back chewing his toy. Next minute he stood on all fours, playing tug and pull with it. Possable while being entertained by her beloved pet thought to herself. *It is amazing how a simple pleasure of a toy can bring so much joy to an animal.*

Possable went back to sit near the tree and placed the three beautifully wrapped gifts beside her. She started with the largest box wrapped in gold. To her surprise, it was lovely formal olive green dress, with a sweetheart neckline, a fitted knee-length bodice with ruffle details. It also had gold straps with a sexy, back cut-out. She was so excited that she spun herself around a few times while holding unto the dress. Jordan watched her from a distance in a confused state, but then went back to his merry moment. Inside the silver box was a pair of sparkling apple, green shoes and a 3-piece expensive looking fine jewelry gold set. Possable let out a loud shriek of happiness that troubled Jordan, who came over to make sure she was fine. Jordan barked twice to get her attention. Possable kneeled down and gave him a kiss on his head letting him know that she was okay. Distracted for a moment by his other chew toy, Jordan picked it up and took it over to be next to his gingerbread stuffed toy.

"Wow! I can't believe Mrs. Fox. She is the best. I love her, I love her. I love her."

Overwhelmed by the other two gifts, Possable felt a little hesitation in opening the last red box. She thought about the old adage that says, "Good things come in small packages."

Instead she reached for the card, opened it, and began to read it.

Chapter 21

Dear Possable,

I hope you enjoy your gifts. I would have loved to see your reaction. I hope you find peace before this year comes to an end. If I had things my way, we all would be spending Christmas together, but unfortunately life does not always give us what we want. It's nice to know that the things that matters most such as: family, love, joy, peace, and the love of Christ are priceless gifts that continue give even after the holidays. I want you to know that I am here for you and that I love you always. I wish you genuine happiness and prosperity with whomever you choose to spend the rest of your life with. I have a funny feeling that it's going to happen sooner than you think. Furthermore, I am also glad you forgave the young man in prison that took your dad's life and forgave yourself in the process. That revelation came in the time it was meant to come; therefore, creating you into this woman, who has so much to share and give back to others. Do continue to be a blessing to those you meet along the way. With all that being said Merry Christmas sweetie and see you in the New Year.

Love Always,
Carol Fox

P.S. Now is the time to pursue your dream.

Possable was moved by the card as she embraced it and cried softly. She knew what Mrs. Fox meant by pursing her dream. She brought it up a few times in conversation with her.

The next day the forecast was calling for a 3:00 p.m. snowfall. Possable knew at that moment the date with Alex will have to be postponed. Shortly after, Possable received a phone call from Alex asking if she still wanted to go through with the plans for later in the evening. Possable told Alex that it will be best to do it at a later time, but Alex begged to differ. He told her that he wanted to see her and if that took driving to her place in the snow to do so, then that was a good enough reason. Possable laughed out loud and shook her head. She then told Alex that he was crazy. He answered her by changing the subject. He asked did she have a particular wine that she enjoyed. She said her favorite was a white wine called "Asti Spunmati." He suggested that they meet at six instead, Possable agreed.

An hour later the house was immersed in the aroma from the food Possable was preparing. Jordan took notice of the smell as he came into the kitchen. He hoped to find something on the floor to eat. The table was set with exquisite china. There was an elegant, red satin tablecloth and a runner in the middle of the table which had sparkling ornaments in silver, gold, and blue. Sitting on top of the runner was a three-tier reindeer candleholder. Two tall synthetic beautiful Evergreen topiaries stood 40 inches high on opposite sides of the fireplace. It gave an extra ambience to the holiday décor. As an added touch, an artificial poinsettia was placed on the coffee table in the living room. As much as Possable loved live plants, she couldn't keep them in the house because of Jordan's allergies. However, come spring time she was planning to plant a small garden in front of her home. Now all that Possable was waiting on was the macaroni and cheese baking in the oven. She checked the kitchen; it read 5:15 p.m.

She had to start getting ready. As she went up the stairs to her bedroom she thought about maybe wearing the dress that Mrs. Fox gave her would be a good idea. The occasion called for something special and lovely. That's exactly how she felt. Moments later Possable came downstairs looking graceful and stunning in the dress. She was also wearing the jewelry gift set with matching earrings, bracelet, and a Y-shape necklace.

Placing the dinner rolls in the oven, she got a call from Alex letting her know that he was about 15 minutes away. She started feeling nervous because it has been three years since she has been on date. Most improbable was the fact she felt comfortable enough to invite Alex for dinner especially since she and Jordan had just settled into their new home. Possable was anticipating spending time with Alex, that's why she felt compelled to cook dinner.

Ten minutes later the "Jingle Bells" melody chimed throughout the house when the doorbell rang. Jordan responded with a few barks. Possable loved the fact that Jordan always alerted her whenever someone was at the door.

Chapter 22

Although Possable presumed it was Alex, she still made certain looking through the peephole. What a gentlemen indeed, she thought to herself. He had in one hand a bouquet of white roses and in the other a bottle of wine. Possable quickly tucked away her smile, unlocking the door.

"Hello, Alex."

"Good evening, Possable. You look exceptional. These are for you."

"Thanks," as she kissed him on the cheek. "You are so thoughtful. I must say you don't look bad yourself."

"Thanks, good looks runs in the family."

"No argument from me." They both smiled. Jordan interrupted with a bark.

"Alex this is Jordan. The one who feels he's being ignored here."

"Hey, buddy," Alex said while giving Jordan a couple of pats on the head and rubbing his ears.

Possable told Alex to make his self comfortable after asking for his coat. But, instead he asked to be directed to the coat closet so that he could do it himself. From the looks of the weather outside the snow was coming down heavily, although it was suppose to stop sometime around 11:00 p.m. Alex looked so good as Possable watched him walk from the coat closet and towards her. She led him to the dining room and offered him a seat.

He took notice of everything from the décor of the table and how the dining area was an extension off the huge, country kitchen, to the aroma of the delicious food, from the decorations on the tree, to the warmth of the fire, and yes he was definitely checking out Possable in her lovely dress. She even had a warm glow to her. As a matter of fact he noticed Jordan concentrating and trying desperately to unravel what appeared to be a box of some sort. Possable noticed Jordan too and walked over to see what he had. It was the last red gift box she had forgotten all about. She asked Jordan to release it, but he refused. She repeated once more, but firmly. Jordan obliged and then moved out of the way for her to retrieve it. The first thought that raced through Possable's mind was what she had conjured earlier about how good things came in small packages. Seeing her delay in opening it, Alex came over to offer consolation.

"What's wrong, Possable?"

"Nothing is wrong, just a little nervous about opening this box."

"What do you think it might be?"

"That's just the thing; I am curious, but not sure if I want to find out."

"Let's consider the possibility that it just might be something that can be life changing for you."

"Yeah, I guess. Excuse me; I forget the dinner rolls were still in the oven."

The dinner rolls were a little overdone, but not burnt. Thank goodness.

Alex placed the small red box into his pockets, planning to present it to Possable later in the evening when her nerves relaxed a bit. Just when he was about to take a seat onto the soft plush sofa, Possable mentioned that dinner was ready. In an awkward way again, she felt comfortable just saying that and being around Alex. Despite the fact she knew Alex since they grew up in the same neighborhood; she wanted to find out more of who the man Alex was today.

Alex, along with Jordan, made his way into the dining room once more, but this time candles were lit creating a glow to the already inviting atmosphere. He noticed that both the wine bottle and roses were on the table. Possable offered to serve him, but he refused. He insisted that she take a seat and allow him to serve her. She was smitten by his gentle and caring approach. This type of treatment was something she could get used too; perhaps even get spoiled a little. Once Alex served them, he said a short prayer and then popped the cork of the wine and poured. Possable took mental notes on all that Alex was doing and thought this man is incredible and how she wanted to learn more about this intriguing man. Jordan stayed in the kitchen eating his share of dinner in the form of dog food. In the middle of dinner Alex reached inside his pocket and took out the red box and handled it to Possable. Looking ever more surprised than before, Possable accepted the gift and placed it in the middle of the table next to the wine bottle.

"Possable, tell me why don't you want to open the box?"

"No particular reason. I'm okay." From the expression on her face, it did not appear that way. "Can you open it instead?"

"*Me?* The gift was intended for you. Whoever the gift is from he or she went out of their way for you to have it. It's only fair that you do the honors." He took Possable's hand into his hand, strokes it, and gently kissed it. He then stood to take his dishes into the kitchen. When Alex returned, he noticed that the box had moved from being next to the wine bottle to the edge of the table beside Possable. To help alleviate the tension he sensed was building in Possable, he deviated from the whole thought and changed subjects.

"Have you thought about what your New Year's Day resolution will be?" He could think of several, but just one main one came to mind and that was to ask Possable's hand in marriage. Although time and space had been between them before; however, he felt a strong bond with her. He knew in his heart, she was the one he wanted to spend the rest of his life with, build with, have children with, and be together to share so many wonderful experiences throughout the years to come.

"I am considering returning back to school to pursue my doctoral. I am hoping it will augment my career with KG Marketing. We will be opening a new KG Marketing in Chicago sometime next year and my boss discussed with me how he plans to relocate to the area once it finally does open. Mainly, he wants to be close to his daughter, Melanie. She will be attending college in the fall at the University of Illinois to study veterinary medicine. Melanie has always been a natural when it came to caring for animals more specifically domesticated ones such as dogs, cats, and horses; so why not pursue a career doing what you love?"

"Wow! Before you know it people will be addressing you as Dr. Possable Johnson. Has a nice ring to it. That's great that your boss will be close to his daughter. I especially like the fact you're considering going back to school. I want you to do so; it means so much to me knowing you are happy and successful in all that you pursue for yourself." He wondered if he said a mouthful and if it came across to lame.

"Alex it's nice to know I have your seal of approval, but I am just considering it for now. Where my heart is really at is....." she just abruptly left it at that.

"What's wrong? What lies in your heart?" He hoped in some small measure he was in her heart along with whatever she wanted to say.

"It's kind of silly, let's just forget about it, okay?" The avoidance made Alex even more curious to find out more, but he respected her decision to leave it alone, at least for now.

Along with what she had to say; he also wanted to find out what was inside that special little red box as well. To change the conversation, Possable asked if he wanted dessert because they were going to have Boston Crème Pie, one of her favorite chocolate treats. Together they cleared the table and loaded the dishes into the dishwasher. Nearby the fireplace, Jordan had fallen asleep and was snoring soundly. Possable smiled as she sat on the sofa with the dessert plate in her hand. Alex sat next to her along with his dessert plate watching as Possable indulged herself with each forkful she put into her mouth. Realizing it was 11:00 p.m. already, Possable unplugged the Christmas tree and the only glow throughout the lower-level of the house was from the fireplace. Settling back down on the sofa, she brought over the wine bottle and poured more into their glasses and handed one to Alex.

"You really like the wine?"

"I really do. I told you that it's one of my favorite. Normally, around the holidays I enjoy drinking Peach Schnapps, but I was in the mood for wine."

"I would have bought both had I known. I want you to have the things you enjoy."

"I appreciate your thoughtfulness, but I am fine."

"Are you sure because you seem to have so much on your mind?" Again Alex didn't want to come across as pushy, but he had to express his concern.

"I have to admit it's a bit mind-blogging that you are reluctant to open a gift and express what's really in your heart. It's almost like you are fighting it."

There was a brief moment of silence between them, with exception of Jordan's snoring. Suddenly, Possable let out a sigh. "I am in a good place in my life right now. I love my career and its great making nice money; I especially enjoy feeling appreciated and admired with those I work with, but by the same token I feel there is so much more in store for me. I am just at a crossroads right now in my life where I want to make changes, but afraid of doing so because everything is going so well for me and the security is there. Does anything I'm saying make sense to you?"

"Yeah, it does. In some way, I can relate when I went through my transition with Erica. After several years of marriage, discovering that Chloe was never mine was heartbreaking, but we agreed that I would remain a part of her life. Yes, I was uncertain and fearful of the changes to come. I was even more devastated when I lost my job. I felt alone, scared, but thank God I had my family. Because of their love, support, and faith I got through it and I feel greater things are in store for me now second time around."

"Well, the truth is Alex; I want to start my own business, but a bit hesitant."

"What type of business?"

"I have always had an interest in home decorations; it's always been a passion of mine to pursue. I feel kind of silly sharing this will you."

"Don't be, don't ever renege your aspirations. You never know what will come out of them."

"Really, you don't think it's a crazy idea especially now when my company will be expanding?"

"You have such a caring spirit and that's fine you are taking loyalty into considering, but you have to live your life to the fullest. If opening a home décor store is what you want to do and it will make you happy, then go for it. All the particulars with your job and the business will fall right into place. Everything is going to work out fine."

Possable reached out and gave Alex a big hug and kissed him a couple times on the cheeks. Once her excitement settled, she apologized to Alex. He rather enjoyed the affection.

"Alex you are so easy to talk and that's why I love you."

A bombshell just dropped in the room and there was another moment of silence. Suddenly Jordan awoke; feeling the depth of the silence. He exited outdoors through his doggy door.

Alex had a shocked look on his face, "Did you just say you love me, Possable?"

"I'm sorry it just slipped out. It must be the wine." She lied hoping he was convinced, but the truth was she did have strong feelings for him, but she didn't want to be the first to admit it.

"Well, okay, that was unexpected." He knew in his heart she meant what she said because the words were expressed with so much emotion and without hesitation. To change the subject, Alex handed Possable her gift once more.

"I guess I should go ahead and open it because the anticipation is driving both you and me crazy."

"You mean, *you crazy*. I'm fine." Yes, he was fine indeed. She imagined for a minute what it would be like to kiss him. She started to slip into a rapturous thought until he disrupted her drifting mind. "Possable, are you going to open it?"

"Well, here goes. Before I do, I just want you to know I am glad we decided to get together. You're fun to have around."

"I am glad I bumped into you back at my dad's restaurant. It's funny; I never thought I would see you again. I feel so blessed to have another opportunity with you."

Looking deep into each other's eyes, there was a strong connection between them, which was saying it was safe to feel because this time around perhaps the feeling of love was real and profound. The moment seem right as Alex moved in a little closer to Possable and softly kissed her on the lips. At first, she was a little resistant, but at the same time every molecule in her body desired Alex. Alex kissed her gently once more and then Possable gave in and they shared a tender, long kiss. It was so passionate that Possable had wrapped her arms around Alex's neck and he had his arms around her lower back. They paused briefly and then kissed once more, but even more passionate than before.

Chapter 23

On New Year's Eve day, when Possable finally opened the red box and found a silver key. She was perplexed. Buried under the key a piece of paper, she unraveled the paper. It was a map with directions to an address. Confused and excited at the same time, Possable drove to the location. To her amazing discovery, it was the actual building that was for lease that she had told Mrs. Fox about. Just to double-check she was at the right place, she looked the directions once more. Overtaken with so much excitement she dropped the key accidently right before unlocking the door. She took a deep breath, opened the door, and stepped into the building. The best part to this surprise was the location. It sat on the corner of Times Square, New York. She never fathomed that her dreams will be coming together so fast. One question that came to mind as Possable wondered through the building, planning and contemplating ideas in her head was how Mrs. Fox could afford to purchase the place especially since she was on a fixed-income. In addition, from a business standpoint she was thinking what would be the monthly leasing cost, the taxes, and how much insurance will cost. Just when she was about leave, she discovered a card on a countertop, where she thought would be a good spot to setup a computer terminal, cash register, and some sort of business signage. The card read:

Hello Possable,

I am Stacey Harris. Let me first extend to you a friendly, warm welcome and congratulations on your decision to pursue your own business. Being a new business owner is both exciting and scary and requires attention to detail and focus. Mrs. Fox (who is my aunt by the way) asked me to be your facilitator. I will help make this transaction as smooth and organized as possible because we want your "Open House" day to be a success. My expertise is in project management and I understand yours is in marketing. Bringing both our experiences to the table will be an exceptional and rewarding experience. When you receive this card, please give me a call at 212-588-2001. I am excited and looking forward to meet and work with you.

Respectfully,
Stacey Harris

P.S. My services are on the house.

"Yes, thank you Father for the answers to my prayers," was Possable's first thoughts after reading the card. She was overjoyed in tears and had to call Mrs. Fox and express her gratitude wholeheartedly for what she did. Also to learn more of how she did it. Right in the middle of dialing Mrs. Fox on her cell phone, she remembered the last time speaking with her that she will not be available until after the 5th of January. What a bummer, oh how she wished Mrs. Fox was here to witness everything that was going on in her world, but she had to put that thought aside for a moment. Returning to her vehicle Possable dialed Alex's cell to share the marvelous news with him.

"Hello Possable. How are you?"

"How did you know it's me?"

Sarcastically Alex replied, "Well it's called caller ID and it lets you know whose calling before answering it. You should try it out sometimes." They both laughed in sync.

All in less than one breath Possable explained what had happened to her. From opening the box in the morning, to driving to the location, then discovering it is the ideal place for a business, and finding Stacey Harris's card. Alex could hear the excitement in her voice, yet at the same token confused, but trying to make sense to what she was explaining.

"Okay, okay, baby, okay, slow down. I probably only heard and understood about half of what you were saying. Take a deep breath and start over, but slower this time."

Possable paused for a moment to breathe, and then proceeded, but slowly once more.

"Remember the red gift box I got from Mrs. Fox? After opening it, I found a key inside of it along with a map and directions to an address. The map led me to a building space for lease which is right here in Times Square. I need to call a lady, Stacey Harris, and setup a time to meet."

"That's terrific! Did you say a building space?" This is a sign that it's meant for you to pursue your business." Alex hoped she'd see the sign that he was totally into her and that he wants to spend the rest of his life with her.

"Alex. Are you still there?"

"I am here, Possable." He sighed and looks up into the sky.

"What's wrong?" She could sense something from the way he sighed.

"I'm okay." He quickly shifted his mood. "The news came at a perfect time with it being New Year's Eve and I think we should go out and celebrate tonight. What do you think?"

Alex's reply of being okay was not convincing to Possable. She planned on asking him about it later on in the evening.

"That sounds good, but you know reservations are out of the question because everyone and everybody will be trying to secure something to ring in the New Year."

"Let me worry about that. How about I pick you up at around 8:00?"

"That's fine. I'll see you then. Alex whatever is troubling you; I want you to know that I am here, okay? You are important to me and I just want you to know that."

"I know and I am here for you, but really I'm fine. I'll see you tonight. Don't forget to call Ms. Harris and good luck."

"I know you are fine." She giggles behind the statement. "But I am more concerned with whatever is going on inside your heart or troubling your spirit. Listen, I'll see you later on and together somehow we will think of someplace to go."

"Alright then, I'll see you Possable."

Chapter 24

New York was definitely the place to be to celebrate the New Year. Times Square was going to have tourists from all parts of the world visiting. Some folks had planned this special event for months and perhaps be witnessing for the first time the dropping of the crystal ball. Every hotel and restaurant was booked and not even one motel chain for miles had vacancies. Luckily, for Alex he had an inside connection through his cousin, Miguel. Miguel and his wife owned two, luxurious hotels. They have been in the hotel and restaurant management business for a combination of 11 years. One hotel was located in San Francisco and the other right in the heart of Times Square. The view faced the busy streets of Times Square with all the billboard advertisements displayed. The streets were being blocked off because of the concert event later on. Each floor to ceiling window showcased in a light-smoked grey shade making the inside of the restaurant look darker outside than it was. Diners were going to be entertained by: Alicia Keys,

Tony Bennett, Maxwell, Usher, Lady Gaga, Chris Daugherty and a few comedians. The most creative and mesmerizing area of the restaurant was a dance floor in the center which had a ceiling window that captured and reflected the moonlight. This was the perfect place Alex envisioned in mind to propose to Possable. Yes, with just dating for only a week, he didn't care about that or about the massive amount of people who would be there watching. All that mattered was professing his love to Possable and hoped she will happily and lovingly accept.

Alex picked up Possable. She came out in a long, black warm cashmere coat with a matching hat and gloves set. As Alex opened the car door for her, she smiled and kissed him on his cheek and fastened her seatbelt. Alex settles for the kiss on the cheek for now and anticipates one on the lips later. Possable noticed how clean and fresh smelling his car was.

"You do realize we are attempting to celebrate on New Year's Eve. One of the busiest—Alex interrupts her suddenly. "I know, but it's cool. I got it.

"You seem so laidback and nonchalant about all this."

"I am. Just relax."

"Okay." She peered at the window remaining silent. Shortly after, Alex drove to a valet parking reserve area, got out and opened the door for Possable. He extended his hand to assist.

Very surprised she smiles at Alex and he smiles back. They walk together and enter the hotel.

They were greeted by the employees in the hotel as they made their way into the restaurant. Immediately they were seated by a hostess near one of the windows and handed a menu. The view of Times Square was spectacular. The whole atmosphere was so inviting from the vibrant, bold colors, to the arrangements and glow of each table that featured a small, white flickering candle enclosed by a glass. Feelings of excitement exuded from Possable. In fact she was so amazed and comfortable with the arrangement of the restaurant she forgot to remove her coat. When she stood to do so, she revealed a sexy V-neck sapphire fitted long-sleeve cocktail knee-length dress that accentuated her figure. For just a brief moment it seemed like the whole room stood still and all eyes were on this totally amazing, lovely woman standing in front of Alex.

Alex was in awe of how incredibly beautiful she looked and how the dress perfectly complimented her beauty and feminism. Along with the dress, Possable had on black pantyhose and dark, navy pumps with a bow on top. Around her neck was a silver necklace with a blue teardrop pendent with matching blue, teardrop earrings. Alex wondered if he was in heaven or dreaming because she looked like an angel with her hair parted in the middle, with curls at the ends and stopped about shoulder length. Definitely, she was his princess and he wanted to be her knight. After getting comfortable, Possable sat down, and looked at her menu.

"You look so beautiful tonight, Possable. I mean, wow, you are stunning."

"Thank you, Alex. I figured why not bring in the New Year in style?"

"I couldn't agree more, but wow you look so amazing. I swear the whole room just froze with your presence."

"You are exaggerating. Come on. You ready to order?"

He was too busy focusing on Possable then on the menu. "Yeah, I mean what are you going to have?"

"I am indecisive between having a steak or grilled chicken."

"I am going to have a T-bone, with a Caesar salad, and a baked potato."

"That sounds good. Think I'll go with the sirloin steak with mashed potatoes and sautéed vegetables."

The waiter took the orders and brought an expensive bottle of wine.

"Remember besides it being New Year's Eve we are celebrating your soon-to-be-opened business venture."

"Yeah, I am so excited. I am so thrilled. I have all these great ideas just waiting to make them happen. I spoke with Stacey. She's so sweet and we are meeting this upcoming Thursday. I was wondering if you could come along."

"That's good. Will this take place after working hours? Remember I start my first day tomorrow and my hours are 8 to 4."

"Silly, I didn't forget. You have great hours. I don't get out until five. We'll be meeting with Stacey at six."

"I'll be there."

"You being there would mean the world to me."

Having Possable in his life meant the world and everything to him. Tonight he was going to make it a known fact.

The waiter was so robust and energetic in how he balanced the dinner plates and trays simultaneously. One of his colleagues came by to offer assistance on settling the plates. While they were in the middle of their meals, a different waiter came by the table with a vase of 12 lovely, fresh long-stemmed red roses. He said it was a tradition each year at the hotel to select a special lady on New Year's Eve and she was the winner this year. That different guy was Miguel. He knew of Alex's plan to propose to Possable and wanted to make the moment even more special and memorable. Possable was delighted and graciously accepted and thanked Miguel.

"Coming to the stage is Alicia Keys." The crowd gathered at Times Square screamed uncontrollably. Some people in the restaurant got up to dance, some alone, others in pairs.

"That's my girl. I love this song," declared Possable." She was lip syncing and grooving at the same time in her seat.

"Yeah she's cool," remarked Alex. You could overhear the crowd and some people in the restaurant singing-along to the words. Yes, even Possable herself got into the motion of singing. Alex was very surprise.

"I didn't know you could sing, Possable."

"Surprised?" She grinned. "There's a lot to learn about me."

Believing her statement to be true; he just smiled. Progressively throughout the night, the host in Times Square announced one performer after the next. The hotel's restaurant band played a few love ballads that Alex and Possable danced to a couple of times. Alex had to admit it felt good holding Possable in his arms as they slow danced and how he loved the sweet smell of her perfume and enjoyed the closeness of her body close to his. He had to contain himself being around her because she had a way of intoxicating him with each touch. Returning to their table, an announcer came out and said that ten minutes remained until the arrival of the New Year.

Alex started to become a bit nervous as he reached into his pockets to make certain the ring was still there. Another bottle of chilled wine arrived at the table. Possable told the server that they didn't request it. The waiter informed them that it was a gift from Miguel.

"What is going on, Alex? Why is Miguel giving us a free bottle of wine?"

The huge luminous clock in Times Square read 11:55 p.m. Alex slowly stood and walked over to Possable. "Do you trust me?"

"Yes, I do. Why do you ask?"

"I ask because I need to know and hear that from you. You are so special to me and I need you to close your eyes right now, ok?"

A little unsure, Possable trusted Alex wholeheartedly. He guided her to the center of the room and sat her down into a chair.

"Open your eyes baby." To her surprise the whole room was dark except for the glowing coming from the candles on each table and all she could make out was dark faces. The announcer came out and said two minutes until New Year's Day. Suddenly realizing that she and Alex were under a ceiling window which gave the illusion of stars falling down among them and the view of the full moon was breathtaking. She was feeling so many different emotions at that very moment as her heart raced.

"Possable Johnson I am so in love with you. You are the love of my life and I am so blessed to have been given another chance to find you because I have longed for years to be with you. Now that you are here, I just want to love you. I want to be able to wake up with you each morning and be with you each and every night. I want to share my life with you and for you to be the mother of my children. And you will make me the happiest and luckiest man alive if you will marry me and become my wife."

"Oh, Alex I love you so much," she says as tears streamed down her beautiful, brown eyes. "Yes, I want nothing more than to be with you and be your wife."

He puts the 18k white gold diamond engagement ring on her finger. It featured 10 beautifully crafted diamonds which complemented the beauty of the ring. They shared a deep passionate kiss and hugged as Possable's eyes were filled with overwhelming joy. Cheers and applauses fill the room for the happily engaged couple. The announcer came on stage and started counting down the remaining 10 seconds. Everyone from the crowd in Times Square to the guests in the hotel counts along as the crystal ball started to make its way to the top. Then in a blink of a second it happened. New Year's Day arrived and brought with it the emotions of people cheering, shouting, kissing, hugging, sharing cries of happiness and toasting of glasses. Confetti and balloons floated down from every direction on the crowd, landing on the ground. Despite the frigid temperatures, folks were celebrating, strangers became acquaintances, and foes became friends. With the much anticipated holiday celebration, all indifferences were put aside because it didn't matter if you were rich or poor, black or white, man or woman, educated or illiterate. What mattered most was just being alive to witness what some would describe as an once-in-a-lifetime exhilarating experience.

What took place between Alex and Possable that evening in front of witnesses was special and heartwarming. Engagement is a life changing commitment and what a blessing it is to find true love with someone you want to spend to the rest of your life with. The love that Alex and Possable shared that night was magical. Each stroke and touch was more sensual than the last.

Chapter 25

A few months later a pregnant Possable and Alex had a beautiful wedding in late April at Central Park. Twenty guests attended consisting of family and friends. The whole wedding ceremony was magical, like a fairy tale because they had a horse and carriage present. They even announced the exciting news that their baby boy Nathan Alex Reyes would be born on October 25th. The happy couple decided to honeymoon in Puerto Rico.

*   *   *

At KG Marketing, Mr. Rio announced his relocation to Chicago taking place at the end of summer to prepare for the opening of the new KG Marketing office he will be managing. The owner and CEO, Keith Grant himself, promoted Mr. Rio to President of KG Marketing. With the new promotion came with it a generous raise of 25 thousand dollars to his already six figure salary. Mr. Rio accepted the new responsibility with the understanding that the first six months his new schedule would consist of managing the new office in Chicago on Mondays, Tuesdays, and Fridays. The New York office was scheduled for Wednesdays and Thursday and afterwards the New York office would be a monthly visit. With Possable resigning the end of July the decision still had to be made as to who would be the new Director of Marketing. Mr. Rio discussed the possible candidates with Possable. She recommended that the new responsibility be entrusted to her protégé, Angela Bello. The recommendation was highly regarded as Angela would be graduating in June with her MBA from the NYU.

Chapter 26

Stacey and Possable have been diligently coordinating and preparing for the much anticipated grand opening of "Home Creations" for the Labor Day weekend. Stacey was planning to be there to offer moral support and assistance.

With the autumn season being right around the corner, the banners, comforters and linens were chosen and ordered well in advance. Outside the store was a canopy advertised with the business name and there was a signage displaying the business hours from 9:30 a.m. to 5:30 p.m. Monday through Saturday. The interior colors were bursting in fiery red, apple greens and chocolate browns. Moreover, the attractive track lightening and light fixtures created an inviting and warm-fuzzy environment. There were two beautifully decorated beds in the latest styles that invited anyone to climb in and cozy up underneath. Six banners displayed ideas on window treatments, bedding sets with extra pillows, contemporary futons with soft throw pillows, area rugs in a variety of patterns and rich colors, kitchenware, and bath accessories. Shelves were easily accessible and organized with various decoration items. Over top of the countertop had a huge sign with the business name and just below it were two cash registers. Behind the countertop were built-in shelves to house wrapping paper, tape, gift boxes, and along with several assorted bags. With the extra space, Possable contoured the idea to showcase the various decorating themes into a replica of an apartment model next door to the main floor. Customers could take a tour of the whole showroom by entering through the French doors which lead to a showroom. It featured a furnished living room, a dining room with an exquisite cherry wood dinette set, a bathroom with window pane mirrors, a bedroom that had a walk-in closet and a wall display of décor candles. An absolutely, inviting fully-equipped kitchen with plenty of cherry wood cabinets, a refrigerator, an electric stove, and cherry wood island in the center. There was a mural giving the illusion of an outside patio furniture set surrounded by grass, plants, and a few trees.

The store was coming together beautifully and Possable could not have done it without Stacey's assistance; indeed she was a blessing.

As a marketing incentive to boost customer's retention on opening day, a five percentage coupon would be given to use for their next shopping experience.

Others decisions included Possable pursing the business full-time and Alex would continue to work at Liriano & Associates' LLP, but she had to hire a full-time and a part-time assistant sometime in September before the birth of the baby. Possable thought hiring Stacey as an assistant would be excellent, since Stacey mentioned her contract with a private developer was ending and she wanted a job that offered more stability. A few days later Possable discussed the assistant position with Stacey and she happily accepted. Possable and Stacey negotiate a starting salary of $50,000 with sales bonuses contingent on future growth down the road.

Chapter 27

It was Possable's last day with KG Marketing and the employees gave her a baby shower and farewell party. There were two super-size bouquets of flowers, a farewell banner sign, and balloons that decorated the office in her honor. The event was catered again by the same caterers from the holiday party last year. Mr. Keith Grant himself attended and brought her a gift wrapped in royal blue with a Hallmark card that had inside of it a $500 American Express gift card. Among the lovely and expensive gifts, were also baby gifts meant for Nathan's arrival. There were sentimental farewell greeting cards, gift cards. E-mails, phone numbers, hugs and kisses were exchanged in the mix. Possable always thinking business-wise handed out her business cards to all and told them she hoped to see everyone at her spectacular grand opening Labor Day weekend. She invited them to a least bring a friend along. They all laughed.

Keith brought a karaoke machine and hooked it up to one of the computers. He volunteered to sing a hit song by "The Supremes." He started to get into the music bobbing his head. He even creatively made up his own version adding Possable's name to the lyrics. Enjoying the entertainment everybody laughed and clapped. There were other singing hopefuls who took the microphone and say old school jams from artists such as: Aretha Franklin, Whitney Houston, Sade, Tina Turner and even Michael Jackson. The fun and entertainment continued on for about another hour and then folks started preparing to go home.

Before everyone left for the evening, Possable thanked everyone for the generous gifts once more. Emotionally she thanked Melvin and Keith for having faith in her for all these years and for giving her the opportunity at KG Marketing and that she was going to miss them terribly. Mr. Rio had tears in his eyes as he embraced Possable and kissed her on the cheek.

Mr. Grant shared a short sentiment of his appreciation of having Possable onboard his team and for leading them successfully and consecutively for the past three years. He ended with a final note that she would be missed, but wished her much success in her new business venture. Possable still emotional announced the successor of her position as Marketing Director to Angela Bello. Cheers and applause surrounded the room as Angela graciously and emotionally accepted the new position. She received firm congratulatory handshakes from Keith, Melvin and one finally from Possable Reyes. One by one all the other employees congratulated her. The office was empty shortly after with exception to the cleaning crew.

How amazing it is to see God's blessings definitely bestowed upon Possable, Angela, and Melvin. These three individuals all of whom had different lives, yet were crossing into new pathways at the same time.

Epilogue

Three years later Home Creations was thriving and grossed close to 400k annually. With another location opening in Philadelphia, Stacey Harris was the on-site manager.

Alex finally obtained his CPA license and was promoted to Finance Director at Liriano & Associates, LLP. Marriage and love between Alex and Possable was still blissful and going strong. They were still crazy about each other. They are expecting their second baby due in May. This time around it was a girl and her name would be Alessandra Raquel Reyes.

Nathan now three years old was excited about becoming a big brother because every day he would rub his mommy's belly and told his sister he loved her.

Occasionally Possable got together with Mr. Rio and Angela to have lunch and play catch up with their lives.

The wonderful Carol Fox, now Nathan's godmother, still lived in Canada. She would visit each year around the holidays and spend it with Possable and the family.

Brandon completed his master's degree and followed in his daddy's footsteps. He is now a middle-school principal.

Yolanda was still working as a real estate agent. She and Eric got married. The small wedding reception was held at the same church that Rev. Carter still ministers at.

Sometimes Possable reflects on the time Rev. Carter accompanied her to the prison and how he encouraged her to forgive Jimmy. When she did, her life has changed dramatically.

After Jimmy claimed Christ in his life and heart, he joined Rev. Carter's prison ministry and completed his sentence. Today he has a counseling degree and finds the upmost joy in working with troubled youth boys. In his spare time, sometimes he accompanies Rev. Carter to the same prison in which he was once imprisoned. Furthermore, Jimmy's baby brother, Justin is in his first year in medical school.

One afternoon at the neighborhood park, Jordan's bark led Nathan and Possable to a tree where they discovered a young limping beagle puppy bleeding badly from an open wound. Feeling nothing but empathy she immediately phoned Alex and they drove the scared and injured dog to Jordan's vet clinic. That evening they brought the beagle home. He was so weak and heavily medicated that the vet insisted on much needed rest to recuperate. Both Nathan and Jordan were so concerned that they stayed by him. "Mommy I like doggie and me sad," said Nathan.

"Yes, baby. I know you do. I think he will be okay." Suddenly the kitchen radio played a familiar song. Possable remembered how much her dad loved that song. In that moment she thought about her dad and how she wished he was there to see his grandson and meet Alex. Oddly, a whisper filled the room that said, "I am here now and I have always been with you. I love you so much, Possable."

She felt a gentle embrace as she closed her eyes and whispered back, "I love you too daddy."

"Mommy, I Nathan not daddy."

She opened her eyes and smiled. She hugged little Nathan and miraculously afterwards the beagle woke up and began walking normally. He ran immediately into Possable's arms and licked little Nathan's cheek. At the very moment Possable knew and felt that her father's spirit was in that puppy.

Alex was in the kitchen preparing dinner but came over to see what the commotion was all about. He too was extremely surprised to see the beagle recovered and so energetic. Jordan barked and ran around the room a few times to express his contentment as well. A few weeks later they adopted the beagle as a part of the Reyes' family and named him Cooper after Possable's dad.

"With God all things are possible."

Matthew 19:26